Cherry Weiner Literary Agent

28 Kipling Way
Manalapan, NJ 07726
(732) 446-2096
Fax: (732) 792-0506
Email: Cherry8486@aol.com

HOT LEAD, COLD HEART

His Honor Newland Pontiff III, late of Exeter Territorial Prison, presides over Cayuse Falls and his vast tract of land. He has ambitious plans for the town, but a demon from his past looms on the horizon . . . Mason, mankiller and vigilante hero, has come to settle one last score with the man who'd wronged the famous 'killer of killers'. Nothing will stop him from seeing this last mission through to its end — an end he knows he won't survive.

MATTHEW P. MAYO

HOT LEAD, COLD HEART

Complete and Unabridged

LINFORD
Leicester

First published in Great Britain in 2008 by
Robert Hale Limited
London

First Linford Edition
published 2009
by arrangement with
Robert Hale Limited
London

British Library CIP Data

Mayo, Matthew P.
   Hot lead, cold heart.- -
(Linford western library)
1. Western stories.
2. Large type books.
I. Title II. Series
823.9'2–dc22

ISBN 978–1–84782–890–3

Published by
F. A. Thorpe (Publishing)
Anstey, Leicestershire

Set by Words & Graphics Ltd.
Anstey, Leicestershire
Printed and bound in Great Britain by
T. J. International Ltd., Padstow, Cornwall

This book is printed on acid-free paper

For my brother, Jeffrey

1

Mason knew he'd have to stop soon. But not yet. This night the idea of making camp — of unsaddling and hobbling the horse, building a fire, preparing food — held little appeal. He wanted to keep riding, though knew he'd pay for it the next day with a stiff back, a sluggish head, and an irritated horse who had an annoying tendency to nip an arm, leg, or sore backside when he'd had plenty of rest, let alone when he'd been denied a full night's repose.

Still, he'd give it a few minutes more. The increasing dark and shaded coolness of the mixed pine and aspen forest made for pleasant riding. And the thick, spongy layers of years of decaying leaves and needles muffled his horse's footfalls. He liked this sort of travel the best — quiet and comfortable. Must be getting old, he thought, and almost smiled. He reached under his worn black duster and worked a sticky knob of chaw from his vest pocket, flicked lint and crumbs, and carved a thumb-size plug.

As he snapped his knife closed Mason heard a high, ragged yelping to the south-east. He pulled back on the stallion's reins and straightened in the saddle, eyes squinting and head cocked toward the sound. A small critter rustled in the undergrowth off to the right. He shifted, listening, the saddle leather creaked and ratcheted until he stopped moving.

It didn't sound like a coyote's usual yip and wolves weren't inclined to such an uneven, messy racket. In his opinion they were among the more musical of creatures. Of course, he knew most folks didn't share that opinion. He tugged the reins left. It would be his end one day, he knew — too curious by half. Had always been. The horse jerked his head back toward their original direction.

Mason sighed and leaned forward over the saddle horn. 'If you're so smart then how come you're the one carrying me?' Bub's ears perked back and Mason tugged left again. The horse fell into line and Mason chewed the quid, his eyes on the trail ahead, fully alert. It would not do to be bushwhacked so close to the end of his journey.

Mason was a tall man with slab hands and a body built of blocks on blocks, topped with a hard jaw and, despite his long years, eyes still a bright blue, a feature that served to soften and add a deserved aura of intelligence to a physique that would otherwise be written off as that of a brawler, the skills for which he also possessed. But despite his looks and skills and reputation, at that moment he was no more than a lone traveler, curiosity aroused, and seeking assurance that danger was not imminent.

★   ★   ★

Twenty minutes later Mason reached the source of the noise. It had grown dark by then, and though the moon was nearly full the thick trees and summer foliage blotted all but reflected silver tails of moonlight that sliced at random through the dark branches. That was enough for Mason to see the prone form of a chubby naked man, astraddle an old mossy log, bigger around than Burla at the Doubloon Saloon in Denver.

Mason sat still for a few seconds, grunted, then climbed down. A sliver of moonlight glowed like birch bark across a headful of reddish curly hair. Mason bent close, looked him over, and saw the man was tied to the log in this intimate pose with hemp ropes. The man wasn't what Mason would call fat, though for sure he wasn't a working man. He was soft, used to drumming or shop work. What he was doing out here was anyone's guess.

The man's head bobbed like a chicken's pecking grain and he moaned and said something that wasn't a word before dropping his face back to the slimy, mossed surface of the log.

Mason grabbed the hair and looked at the man's face. The band of moonlight angled across the smudged features, but it wasn't enough. He fished in a vest pocket for a kitchen match, popped it alight with a thumb-nail, and held it close to the dirty, stubbled face. He didn't know him. The eyes flickered open and the man screamed. Mason let go of the hair and the head thunked against the log. The man lay still.

Mason mounted the stallion. The horse dipped his head then tossed it high. 'He's none of my affair,' said Mason, nudging the horse with his heels.

Bub neighed and shook his head. The man on the log raised his wobbly head and said, 'Here now, here now, let me up. We've all had our fun but it's time we call it a day. Call it a day . . . ' His face slipped back to the log. Mason

5

heard the clunk and then the soft man's moans.

Sighing, Mason dismounted again and set about making camp. It took him less time than usual because, though it was a mess, this spot had already been a camp. There was a fire pit and enough wood for the evening lay scattered about. Whoever tied the man was gone hours since. Most of the day, he figured. He bent low and palmed the ashes. There wasn't even the memory of warmth in the coals.

★　★　★

The scent of two rabbits roasting on sticks angled over the glowing coals awoke the man again. He lay still, moaning and muttering.

Mason leaned forward and pulled a glistening leg off one carcass.

'Who's that, now? Who's there at my fire?' said the naked man.

Mason ignored him. The man struggled to sit upright and found he was bound to the log on which he lay. 'Well, what is this now? What sort of game are you playing at?' He struggled, jerking his limbs what little distance the ropes allowed. He stopped, his breath ragged, and said, 'Hey now, what game is this? Aren't you going to help me? Cut me loose?'

No response. He struggled, again to no avail, and said, 'I demand you release me. This is — this is outrageous!'

Mason sipped his coffee and said, 'Why should I? You were enjoying yourself fine before I came along.'

'What do you mean?'

'I mean you were like that when I happened to hear your caterwauling a few miles off.'

The man raised his wobbly head again, tried to focus on Mason, and shook as if to dispel an irksome bee. 'I didn't do this to meself. How could I?'

Mason shook his head and stood slowly. He'd already pulled off his boots and propped them by the fire. He straightened and his knees protested, then his back. He reached the naked man and sliced through the rope down low against the log to avoid cutting him.

'Go easy. You'll be crampy for a bit.'

The man lay there, sagged and sighing, before finally trying to rise off the log. He succeeded in pushing himself up with one arm enough to roll to the ground. He flopped like a sack of wet corn meal and lay there moaning. It took him another ten minutes to raise himself to a sitting position against the log. He rubbed his arms and legs and slowly picked at the knotted ropes still attached to him.

'Well, don't you want to know who I am?' His head weaved back and forth as he spoke.

'No.'

'All right then, I'll tell you,' said the little man, still rubbing his wrists. 'I am Thaddeus Entwistle Donleavy. Purveyor of the Professor's Own Finest Nostrums, Tinctures, Talcs . . . ' His voice grew loud, then he said, in a near-whisper, 'But my dearest friends all call me Irish.'

Mason kept eating.

'And your name is?' said the man. Mason stared into the fire as if alone, working the last morsels of meat off a leg bone. 'And you are?' repeated the little man, his eyebrows arched, his head steadier than before.

Mason picked at his teeth with a fingernail.

The little naked man drew his legs up in front of himself and shivered.

Mason set down his tin cup on a rock, and pulled his saddle bags closer. He rummaged in one and pulled out a long underwear one-piece, more pink than red, so old and worn was it. He tossed it to the little drunk and said, 'Put that on and eat. Before I finish it all.'

The little man looked down at the suit in his lap and said, 'I'm not hungry.'

'Well, I am. And seeing you naked is almost enough to put me off my feed.

Now get dressed.' The big man's tone was such that even through his drunken haze the little man complied. At last he stood, using the log for support. He grunted and wobbled and fell over twice as he pulled at the suit. The underwear sagged in all the wrong places and the legs and sleeves were far too long. He managed both sleeves and one leg and then passed out, snoring against the log.

Mason looked over at him, pulled his wool blanket over his shoulder, and tipped his hat over his eyes.

★ ★ ★

The new day's first light crawled through the trees as Mason toed the little drunk. 'Get up.' Mason levered a boot under a sagged arm. He lifted and rolled the man over, face up. The little man moaned and an eyelid flickered. He moaned again, then pushed himself up, swaying on all fours like a small, hairless bear. He squinted at the rising sun and a donkey face stared down at him. The little animal looked as if it knew something he didn't. An ear twitched.

'Nubbin?' said the man on the ground, squinting one eye at the beast. 'I guessed that mite-infested soap sack was yours.'

The man recoiled and fell into the log. 'Who said that?' He focused on Mason, who was busy snugging a bedroll behind the cantle of his saddle. Mason looked at him and shook his head.

'There's a little coffee left. Drink up and be quick about it. I'm leaving.'

'What?'

Mason crossed to the other side of the horse and flipped open his saddle bag. 'Hurry up with my cup. And for God's sake, finish dressing yourself.'

The little man pushed himself upright and looked down at his half-nude, debris-covered body. With great care his two shaking hands groped the long underwear. 'Where's me possessions?

What have you done with them? And Florence? Where's Florence?'

Mason looked up. 'Who? Is she your wife?'

Despite his obvious infirmities, the little man laughed. 'Ha! Me wife. Did you hear that, Nubbin? He thinks Florence is me wife.' The donkey twitched an ear. 'Now why would you be thinking I'd be married to a mule?'

Mason shook his head and said, 'Enough palaver.' He picked up the tin cup of coffee resting on a rock by the already doused fire. He was about to toss the liquid on the trampled grass of the clearing when the little man grabbed his hand and said, 'Ah, ah, ah, I'll drink that, thank you kindly.' And he gulped it down. Mason stared at him as if he had greeted him in a foreign language. Then he grabbed the cup from the man and stuffed it in his saddle bag. He mounted Bub and steered the horse around the fire ring.

'Where are you going?'

Mason kept riding.

'Hey, hey there, mister. What's happened here? Where are you going?' The small man lifted the front of the long underwear to his nose and said, 'And where in God's name did this thing come from? It smells as if it's been in the bottom of a bag of dung.'

Mason's jaw muscles worked harder and he urged Bub out of the clearing.

'Hey there. Wait a minute. I'm not through with you, mister! You can't just rob a man and then leave!' He shook a pudgy little fist at the retreating form of the big man on the horse and was startled to find that the man stopped. Man and horse sat like stones in the middle of the rough trail.

The little Irishman looked around himself and saw nothing but a couple of cut ropes flopped on the ground near the log. And beside him stood Nubbin the donkey, his sad face looking downward at the trailing ends of his rope bridle. Nothing else. No Florence, none of Nubbin's packs, none of his own gear, nothing. All gone. He retrieved one of the ropes and tied it about his waist, looped twice. Then he grabbed Nubbin's reins and walked toward the man. When he was ten feet away Mason turned in his saddle and said, 'No one's ever called me a thief to my face and lived.'

The little man swallowed hard and nodded, what little color that had risen in his cheeks drained away once again.

'Now as for your gear. You're looking at it. I found you tied to that log yonder, drunk and howling at the moon. This morning down by the stream I found that big-eared rat you're leading. Other than a mess of empty and broken tincture bottles all over the woods hereabouts, I found nothing. Except lots of hoofprints leading away from here. Looks like you had company.' He turned and faced the man. 'Any of this coming back to you?'

The little man's face collapsed in thought.

Mason turned around in his saddle and urged the horse forward. 'Keep the union suit,' he said over his shoulder. He touched Bub's ribs lightly with his heels and they loped into the trees. 'It was getting a tad ripe for my bags.'

'But you can't leave me here!' said the little man. This time his words had no effect on the retreating shape. He followed, tugging on the donkey's reins, and wincing as he stepped on one bony twig after another. 'Hey, fella! Wait for me!'

He held one foot and balanced for a few moments on the other. The donkey stared at the ground as if embarrassed at his life having come to this. Then the little man fell over. He stayed there, holding his feet like a monkey.

'Have you never seen the likes at all?' The donkey's ear twitched. 'I'll never catch up to him without shoes.' He looked back toward the log and campfire, the spot he'd called home for the past few days until . . .

'That's it, Nubbin. Those thieves of yesterday. Ah, but I've been a fool. It's all coming back.' He rubbed his face

15

with shaky hands and said, 'Oh God, what am I to do? Gone, it's all gone I tell you. They even took the clothes off me back.'

He straightened and looked about himself, 'And there I was helping them with their ailments. Free of charge, with me finest nostrums. Oh the Professor's not going to like this one little bit, so he's not.'

He slouched again and thumbed his temples. 'My only chance for survival lay with that one there and I offended the man so badly he up and left. I'd make amends, so I would, but without shoes I'll never catch the poor soul.'

The donkey nosed the sparse grass poking through the mat of pine needles and the movement caught the little man's eye. 'Unless we can come to some arrangement, my good friend.' He rested a hand on the donkey's bristly mane. The donkey flicked an ear.

2

'Stropworth, I can assure you that there will never be another deal like this for quite some time to come.' The Honorable Newland Pontiff the Third, known to most citizens of Cayuse Falls as Judge, spoke while gazing out over his town's main street through the window behind his massive desk. He knew his turned back perturbed the rancher and he also knew that, as the wealthy and self-appointed representative of what he considered the best interests of the town, Skin Stropworth was the one man who could put a stop to his delicate plans. The little fat judge clenched his teeth tight together, forced a smile, and turned to face the rancher.

Skin Stropworth was a tall, thin man with dangling hands that looked out of place no matter what he did with them. Mostly he let them hang at the ends of his sticklike arms, swaying there under his forward-curving body. Pontiff's initial impression of the man six years before had been that of a big ol' vulture, and that first impression stuck.

Skin's eyes were dark like agate and he hardly ever blinked. He had the ruddy complexion of a man who spends his time in the out of doors, and while that itself was no crime, it didn't make Pontiff feel any better about his own pinker, softer self.

Truth was, Pontiff didn't like looking at the man. He wished he would go away. Coming in every day and hounding him wasn't getting the letter from the railroad here any faster.

Looks aside, Skin's most abiding and notorious feature was cheapness. Rumours abounded, and Pontiff doubted very few of them, as to the limits of Skin's frugality. So far, none had been disproved. All this did not help Pontiff, he knew, because he was obliged to deal with the man at every twist and turn in the road to Cayuse Falls' eventual fortune.

Trying to convince this land-wealthy rancher, who appeared to be the town's sole representative in the matter of the railroad, that spending a dime to make a dollar was sound business practice, was, Pontiff was nearly ready to admit, impossible work. But like it or not, this carrion eater of a man was his cross to bear. Pontiff sighed inwardly and looked at the long nose with its perpetual quivering drip at the end, and said, 'Trust me, Stropworth. It will be well worth the wait. Patience is a virtue.'

'That's not the first time I heard that from you, Pontiff.'

Pontiff turned back to the second-floor window behind his desk. He straightened his back, his eyeline rose above the middle sash. To the far right he made out the last of the scaffolding on the façade of this very building, his courthouse.

Aside from his office and the court-room, which also would double as the town meeting space, final construction on the building — mostly finish work — was progressing slowly, as funds became available. He'd convinced the townsfolk to invest in their municipal building if they wanted Cayuse Falls to stand any chance at all of becoming what he liked to think of as the 'Washington of the West.' It had taken six long years of convincing them of it, week after week, but with the impressive building nearly complete, Pontiff felt confident that they were seeing what he had in mind from the first day he had arrived.

And it was all his. Every inch of it. In a manner of speaking, anyway. And while reappointment wouldn't guarantee that it keep rolling along as smoothly as it had these past few years, it might grease the skids enough to throw off the damned hell-hound creditors. All he needed was another two-year stint as Cayuse Falls' mayor and judge, and he was all but guaranteed a lifetime seat on the newly forming regional legislative board. And that, he was confident, would about guarantee a lifetime of appointments to senate seats and maybe even a governorship. And after that, who knew?

He couldn't have timed it better if he had planned it. Though everything that had happened these past six years *had* been planned, of course. He'd had plenty of time to lay out every minute of the second half of his life from that rat-infested hole of a cell at Exeter Territorial Prison he'd shared with McCorkle and the Jug, a man so named because of his massive ears.

A corner of Pontiff's mouth twitched as he thought of the fickle ways of human nature. He knew better, of course. He knew there was nothing planned in the natural world. Life wasn't any more fickle than he was evil. Contrary to what Stropworth said about him, Pontiff genuinely wanted to serve the best interests of the people he represented. And if they were truly grateful, then they would not begrudge him the material wealth normally associated with one who holds a powerful position.

Pontiff ran a finger back and forth on the slick, polished mahogany of the windowsill. 'There is nothing I can say or do to convince you of anything you don't want to be convinced of, Skin. But I have to say that your lack of faith in me and in my abilities to get things done in this town — and let's face it, this town wasn't much of a town before Newland Pontiff the Third rolled on in — is not a little troubling.'

The large rancher's forced smile became a hard-set line. A jaw muscle worked, and those veined eyes seemed to sharpen. 'There are some of us who aren't necessarily convinced of your infallibility, Pontiff. You may have the rest of the town feeding from your fat pink hands, but not me and not my boys.'

'And how about your daughter, Susan . . . McCorkle? Hmm?'

'Don't you dare bring up my daughter. It's not my fault she married your personal guard.'

Newie sighed, perhaps longer than was necessary. 'He's the town marshal, Skin, and we happen to have to work together and we also happen to get along well. Nothing more.' Pontiff pulled out his desk chair and sat down heavily. A wheeze of air escaped from the leather seat cushion. He coughed. The large rancher stared at him. Like a damned prize bull, dumb but dangerous, thought Pontiff, turning his attention to his desktop.

'When?' said Skin.

Pontiff looked up from his papers — deeds and transfers he'd already signed, but the hick rancher wouldn't know the difference. 'When what?'

'When does the authorization arrive from the railroad company? It's the one question everyone in town wants an answer for. These people have trusted you. Too much, in my estimation. Don't you let them down, or there'll be hell to pay, Pontiff. Hear me well.'

Pontiff put down the papers and said, 'We've been over this, Stropworth. I expect it any day. Why, I wouldn't be surprised if it didn't come in on the next stage. Let's see, it's Monday morning, so that would be,' he squeezed the red tip of his tongue between his teeth and looked at the ceiling with narrowed eyes. 'Wednesday's stage. Or they've assigned a special dispatch rider for the sole purpose of delivering that document to me. Either way, we're in good shape. Bound to have it in hand this week.' He replaced his half-spectacles on the end of his nose and focused on the top sheet in front of him.

The big man plunked his brown broad-brim hat on his head and said, 'Pontiff, you're either a damn good liar or you're genuinely not worried. And if you're not worried, you should be.' Three long strides took him to the big door. He pulled it open, then leaned on the knob. 'You know,' he said, half-smiling at Pontiff. 'My guess is you're a good bit of both.' Before the door shut, Pontiff heard him say, 'Wednesday it is, then.'

Pontiff watched the door close, clunk shut. He dragged his teeth across his bottom lip, worked his spectacles' wire curls off his ears, and tossed them on the desk. He ground his knuckles deep into his eyes a long time and sat there behind his desk in his massive office. 'By Wednesday.' he said aloud. 'One way or another, I will have that paper.'

He stopped rubbing his eyes. 'The cheapest rancher in the world breathing down my neck, still no paper from the railroad's head office, and Mason could show up any second. That's all I need.' He opened his eyes. Maybe that is all I need, he thought. He sat up in his chair, stared at the closed door, and almost smiled.

3

The flickering shadow of a low-flying, red-tail hawk caused Mason to look up. From the angle of the sun, pinned and wavering in a steel-blue sky, he judged the time at a few hours past noon.

He was passing through the marshy bottomlands tailing out of a beaver bog, the water well below Bub's belly, though Mason kept his stirrups high. He had no intention of wearing wet boots any longer in his life than he had to. In his youth he had plenty of days — even weeks, it seemed — spent with sopping feet, his socks sodden and useless, and his boots, painful at the best of times, curling and plain ornery from constant wettings and dryings. No sir, he'd earned these decent boots and the dry feet in them.

He made it to the far side of the bog and reined up on a nice knob, just right for Bub to graze. He'd rest for a bit, give the stallion some time to relax. He knew he should be in more of a hurry to get to Cayuse Falls, still two days of easy riding from here, but since he left that tenderfoot this morning he'd hankered for a proper cup of coffee, not that rushed pot he'd made do with.

That was a situation he'd not care to be in any time soon. What a mess that little Irish fool got himself in. Obviously robbed when he was blind drunk. And whoever heard of a drummer being that far up in the hills? And so near Ute territory. If they weren't stirred up enough by Washington's latest damn shenanigans, then that little Irishman sure would tip the scales.

Mason shook his head and smiled, despite himself. He'd freed him, retrieved that little donkey, and given him some-thing to wear. That was more than most men up here would have done. And a damn sight more than any Indians would do for him. He's lucky he got that. Gave him a fighting chance at least.

He'd make his way down out of the mountains and stumble on a settlement. Men like that always came up with luck when they needed it most. Besides, somehow Mason didn't think the little drunken Irishman was all that helpless.

He set his gray, sweat-stained hat on the grass beside him and checked the coffee. Nearly ready.

'Dumb like a fox,' he said aloud, chuckling as he set the pot on the stones by his little blaze. And then Bub perked his ears forward and raised his head. A second later he nickered a low warning. Mason flattened out against the grass, drew his Smith & Wesson .44 American, and cocked it slow. He raised his head enough to peer over the tall grasses rimming the flow.

He narrowed his eyes and angled his head left a touch. His right was his better ear, but before he saw anything he swore he heard . . . singing? A lone voice nearly shouting. Who was fool enough out here in the fringe country to — Oh no, it can't be, he thought, and raised his head. Bub nickered and stamped at the grass.

'Tell me all about it,' said Mason. He dropped back to the ground, his cheek touching grass. It was unbelievable. He'd seen some things that could scarcely be swallowed, so odd were they he doubted he'd ever be able to tell them to others, even if he were inclined to saloon storytelling. But this fellow took the starch out of most anything he'd seen to this point in his life. How could he possibly have trailed him? He had no boots and . . .

As if in response to his thoughts he heard a sawing, throaty braying. 'I should have killed that thing when I found it this morning,' he said. Bub looked down at him and nickered.

Mason raised his head again and there, not thirty yards away, across the tailout, sat that confounded Irish tenderfoot straddling his donkey. The little man stared right back at him.

Mason dropped his face to the grass again and gritted his teeth, his eyes wide.

'Hello there, big fellow! It's lucky I found you, though really it wasn't that hard. You left quite a trail. Here I am!'

Mason closed his eyes and said, in a low voice, 'Go away and leave me be.'

'Excuse me, there. Are you hurt? Only if you're not, do you happen to know a good way across this brook? Either I've gotten taller or Nubbin's got a case of the shrinks.' The little Irishman laughed. His swinging feet nearly brushed the ground. 'Did you hear that, Nubbin? Before long I'll be carrying you.'

Mason sighed and stood up, snatching his hat and plunking it in place. He moved to holster his pistol and hefted it for a second, staring under his hat brim at the gawking little man on the donkey. Mason thought better of it and jammed the pistol into its holster. He'd reached to dump the coffee when the little man spoke.

'I'm looking to thank you. And to apologize for earlier accusing you of robbing me.'

Mason looked over at him and sighing, set the pot back on the rock. He rubbed his hand over his beard stubble and, as there was nothing else to do, he sighed again.

'If I could get you to lend a hand with Nubbin. He's a stubborn little thing, so he is.' The Irishman jerked back on the reins, then sawed them left and right, and kicked at the little donkey's ribs with his bare heels. The animal stood, lock-legged at water's edge, and braying louder than before, it raised its entire body, save for the firmly planted front feet, straight up in the air. It gave a mighty twist and Mason watched wide-eyed as the Irishman, equally wide-eyed, arced as if he were diving, straight into three feet of water. Nubbin backed up a step and lowered his head. One ear twitched.

★ ★ ★

'I thank you kindly for the coffee,' said Irish. He looked over at the big man as he sipped from a chipped tin cup. He said it again.

'I heard ya.'

'Well now, what shall I call you? Sure you have a name. Every last one of us has a name. Why, even Nubbin there, humble servant though he be, has a name. Don't you, lad.'

The big man tossed a handful of jerky from his saddlebag into Irish's lap. The little man grunted and jammed a piece into his mouth.

'Easy,' said the big man. 'It's gotta last you.'

Irish slowed down his jaws, but not for long. He jammed a second piece in his mouth. The big man shook his head.

After a few minutes of hard chewing, Irish sat there with a last scrap of jerky in his lap, his bare feet sticking up in the air, and he said, 'Aren't you curious as to how I came to be lashed astride that log?'

'No.'

'Are you sure?'

'Yes.' The big man stood up and dumped the last of the coffee.

'Well,' said Irish, as if invited, 'I'm Thaddeus Entwistle Donleavy, Exclusive Western Salesman for Professor's Own Brand of Liquid Solutions for Everyday Problems. Professor's Own, Purveyor of Lotions, Liniments, Tinctures, Tonics, and Soothing Balms.' He looked up at the big man, who was rummaging in his saddlebag again. 'But you can call me Irish. Everyone I've met since coming to these fine shores has. I don't mind.' He got no response, so he continued.

'I had settled down to a warm fire. Florence, that's me mule, and Nubbin here you've met already, were tied for the night and I had stretched out by the fire, awaiting my supper to heat. Canned goods, I always carry plenty of canned goods with me when I'm traversing savage terrain. When straight out of the shadows dropped an evil such as I have never seen.'

The big man glanced at him, so he kept on talking. 'Three, maybe four, yes, now it's coming back to me. It was four big brutes on horseback stormed me campsite, disturbing the quiet and calm evening, scaring Florence half to her death. It's no small wonder she left us, I'm afraid, for parts unknown. I'm sure she's still running. An excitable creature she is, steadfast and true in her own way, to be sure, but not one to take kindly to surprise. And surprise it was, sir, I can tell you! They rode in, beat me without let up, and I don't mind me telling you I begged for a bit of the Mother Mary's mercy, but they were having none of it. I'm thinking they weren't Christians.' This last he said in a whisper.

The big man stood by his horse, a pair of gray wool socks in one hand, the reins in the other, and stared at Irish, who looked down and continued his tale.

'"What is it you want?' I shouted to the devils. And me a poor peddler and all. 'We want your money and your horses.' Well, I told them I didn't have a horse, just the one excitable mule, long since vanished, and a lowly donkey.' He turned to Nubbin and said, 'No offense meant, lad, but surely you remember the devilish glint in their eyes. I wasn't meself.'

Irish looked up at the big man, who still stood by his horse, his hat pushed back on his head, staring at him. 'Cut to the chase,' he said.

'Right you are, sir, though being Irish I can't say that's an easy task to master. But I'll try, I'll try.' He held up his hands and smiled. 'The fiends rummaged through my meager belongings and helped themselves to the Professor's Own Tinctures and Tonics. What they didn't drink they smashed and what they didn't smash or drink they forced on me. They stripped me down and beat me with clubs and whips. I'm covered all over with savage bruises and marks of the lash. Oh, you'd shudder to know the pain I'm in.'

He hugged his own shoulders and rocked in place. 'Thank the Lord for the Professor's Own marvelous tinctures and tonics. Without them in me system I would surely have expired. But oh, I tell you the very same combination of all those tonics in me system also rendered me helpless. The Lord works in mysterious ways, so he does. I soon lost all ability to speak and soon after I lost the ability in me limbs to hold meself up. They tied me to that log and it was pure agony for what must have been a week of endless days and nights. I was driven insensible by their cruelty. And that's the state you found me in.'

The big man straightened his hat, raised his left foot into his stirrup, and hoisted himself into the saddle. He looked down at the little man and said, 'Nice story. I don't believe it, but it was amusing. Here,' he tossed the pair of large, misshapen wool socks into the little man's lap.

Irish looked at them, then up at the

big man, and said, 'But — '

'I'm heading out,' said the big man.

Irish jumped to his feet. 'You can't! What will I do out here alone?'

'You have fire and a little food. And that donkey.' The big man shook his head and said, 'And there's a town a couple of days' ride that-a-way.' He nodded ahead of him into the trees. 'You'll live.'

Irish watched him ride on for a few silent seconds, then looked down at the socks in his hand, and hobbled up the trail, shouting and waving his arms. The big man stopped. 'Are you a man of the law?' Irish said, panting and resting a hand on the big man's boot.

The big man snorted and shook his head, more for himself than in answer to the question.

'You're not a lawman? Are we headed into trouble?'

'We aren't. You are.'

Irish stopped and said, 'What do you mean?'

The big man looked down at Irish,

the man's dirty hand resting on his boot. Irish pulled his hand away. 'I mean if you keep following me and talking like words are free, then I will shoot you.'

He rode forward, leaving Irish standing behind him, open-mouthed.

Finally, Irish shouted, 'You can't mean that!'

The big man, still facing forward, pulled his pistol, cocked it in one meaty paw, and pointed it back behind him — directly at the little man in his wake.

Irish screamed, covered his head with his hands, and ran back toward Nubbin.

Up the trail the big man shook his head, holstered his pistol, and rode into the forest.

4

A little past midday on Monday, as he crossed the street from Jasper Bros. Smithing and Signs, checking on the progress — or lack of it, as it turned out — on his new 'County Jail' sign, Ripley McCorkle heard a familiar voice from on high say, 'Oh, Marshal — ' He looked up, as did several other people in the street, and saw the judge leaning on his windowsill two floors up. Most of what he saw was belly, wrapped in gray wool layered with a gold watch chain, and the face of his old friend peering from under the raised sash, a too-large cigar pointing like a dark commanding digit from his lips.

The judge smiled, hooked a pink finger around the cigar, said, 'You have a minute, Marshal?' He moved back from the window before Rip answered. Rip's smile faded and he sighed. The few other people in the street smiled at him and Peter Sweeney, the lawyer, actually winked, as if he shared some secret with the lawman. Rip's scowl was wasted as he changed direction and headed to the front doors of the courthouse.

He took in a deep breath and pulled open one-half of the big double-doors. He tried to tread lightly on the stairs but the stairwell was empty at this hour of the day and his steps echoed. The building still wasn't complete. The funds for the finish carpentry had been temporarily shut off. No one seemed to mind, considering the speed with which the town had become the territorial seat so soon after Pontiff arrived. It was rumored the judge had powerful friends back East. Rip never doubted it. In fact, he'd heard so many rumors of late concerning Newie that he wasn't sure he knew the man at all anymore. If he ever did.

He reached the door and looked up at his tan felt hat, smirked, and removed it. He rapped hard on the door with his knuckles.

'Come on in, Rip.'

He entered, careful to ease the door shut just enough so the metal catch clicked softly.

'Have a chair,' said the judge, waving a pink hand toward the two leather chairs in front of his massive desk.

Pontiff waited until the marshal was seated, hat on knee, then said, 'Rip, how long have we known each other?', his eyes still on the worn hat balanced on Rip's knee, the thin hand resting on its crown.

'Well now, Judge, I — '

'It's been a damn long time. Years and years. And let's dispense with the 'Judge' and 'Marshal' designations. I was wrong about that, Rip, and I'm sorry. We're too good ol' friends to use such terms. We know each other, in some ways, better than any wives can know their husbands, better than any brothers can know each other. I've asked myself why this is so. And you know what answer I come back to every time?' He turned from the window and squinted at Rip hard, that same look he got on his face when he wanted everyone within sight to know he was listening, really listening, to a plaintiff plead a case. Rip shook his head, still unsure where this conversation was headed.

The judge almost smiled. 'It's because we've served time in prison together, Rip.' He was nodding his head and had bunched his cheeks up like he did when he was regrettably agreeing with a defendant's case. 'And in my estimation it takes such a tribulation not only to bring men together but to harden them to life's required duties.'

Rip thought this chat was beginning to sound like one of Newie's campaign speeches. As far as he knew he was the only voter in the room, besides the judge himself, of course. But he did apologize, something he'd never heard the judge do before. Rip remembered his father saying that a man who apologizes is not a man. He'd think on that one later.

The judge stopped talking. 'Are you even listening to me, Rip, or am I blowing smoke up my own ass?'

'That I'd pay to see,' said Rip, smiling despite his intention not to have a good time.

'And that's the Rip I know, full of it and dishing it back.' The judge smiled and leaned back in his chair. It creaked and made one strong popping sound before settling. Rip knew his boss's feet were wagging there, not touching the floor. Judge wasn't a tall man but he laid down big, as his father used to say about short, stout brood cows on the little dirt farm he'd grown up on back East. Newie was the only short man he'd ever met who truthfully didn't care about his height. He had that kind of attitude. Rip guessed that was most of what made him so successful.

The pudgy man got up with a grunt and walked over to a sideboard. He pulled a new bottle of MacSwain's Malt from behind a few others and held it up and smiled. Rip was about to protest but the judge turned away, prying the red wax seal from the head of the bottle. Rip heard the satisfying 'punk' of the cork leaving the bottle and two healthy measures of whisky being poured. The judge carried them over, handed one to Rip, and said, 'To the good old days, may they rest in peace. To good old friends, may they always remain that way. And to good times ahead.'

They both sipped and Rip said, 'Thanks, Judge — ahh, Newie.'

'That's the spirit,' said Pontiff, crossing back behind his desk.

And that's when Rip's mind nibbled the edges of a feeling rising in him. A feeling that maybe the judge was leading him along a path again. It had happened that way in the past. And Rip had never been quick enough on the uptake to grab it until he was well along that path, nodding and trying to keep up with the urgings of the judge. But he'd recognized it quicker this time, hadn't he? Maybe he was getting more clever. He sipped the whisky. It burned. He preferred Sully Garvin's own mash. It peeled paint but it was quick and cheap relief at the south end of a long day.

Then he noticed the judge staring right at him.

It was some minutes before the fat man spoke. When he did his voice, always deeper than Rip expected from such a short, round body, cracked the still air of the office like a rifle shot ending a pleasant prairie morning.

'There's a man. A known outlaw. He's headed this way.'

Rip sat up straighter in the chair and looked around him, then back to the Judge. Pontiff smiled. 'Not yet, Rip. Not yet. But he's coming. Sure as we're sitting here, Rip. He's coming to Cayuse Falls.'

'Well, who is he?' Rip set his glass on the edge of the desk. His chair squeaked lightly as he shifted, facing his employer.

Pontiff inhaled and sighed, letting it out slowly. 'It's Mason, Rip.'

Rip knew by the judge's tone and by the slow way he was taking to get around to this that he was either being strung along or he really should know who this Mason was. He stared at Pontiff, the small, deep-set eyes, the soft, pink face of a town man, the mouth almost smiling, waiting . . . And then Rip recalled the name, the posters, and finally the oft-told stories of the man. And then he knew who this Mason was. 'Can't be,' he said, as if his wishing would make it so.

'But it is,' said Pontiff.

Rip sat up straighter in his chair. 'How do you know he's headed this way?'

Pontiff stared at him for a moment, then sipped his drink. He was irritating most of the time, but never more so than now. Rip was about to get up. He did his best thinking when he walked a bit. Apparently the judge did his best when he was sitting down.

'I know someone from Kansas City who last year claimed to have seen him there. Turns out they were right. He'd been holed up, working as a short-haul teamster, a dealer in a gambling house, and a few other things.' He paused, leaning back in the chair and smiling.

Rip stared at him.

The judge rocked forward, his shoes patting the floor, and he grunted. 'Look, Rip, you got to work with me on this one. The notorious outlaw Mason is headed out this way, see?'

Rip nodded.

'And since he's what you'd call a high-profile wanted man, then he's not going to blather all over the territory that he's headed to a no-name place like Cayuse Falls. Follow me?'

Other than thinking the judge had gone barmy, he didn't see what else there was to follow. Rip shrugged, nodded. 'I reckon.'

'Good.' The judge licked his lips. 'So he's on his way here. By horseback, heading in the direction my contact back in Kansas City saw him take, which was due north. That means he's avoiding major travel routes. He'll probably dip down across the western foothills of the Pelarosas, which would land him pretty near Cayuse Falls. I'd say within the next four, five days.'

Rip nodded, folded his arms. 'What have we got that he wants, Newie? It ain't like Cayuse Falls is hoppin' with his sort of victim.'

The judge swallowed and said, 'What do you mean by that, Rip?'

'Well, way I hear it, he's more of a bounty hunter than he is a cold-blooded killer. I know pretty near everybody in town and there's nary a one who'd be on his sort of list.'

The judge licked his lips. 'I have a feeling someone hired him to stop us from getting the railroad contract.' He sat up and said, 'I'd bet the farm that's Mason's plan, sure as daylight.'

Rip knew what the railroad meant to the town. On the other hand, it didn't sound like something Mason would be involved in, not from what he'd heard of the man's dealings.

'So — ' said the judge, leaning back again.

'So?' said Rip.

'So, dammit man,' said the judge, pitching forward again. The chair shrieked like a frightened child. 'So he's never going to make it here, Rip. Right?'

'And why's that?' Rip squinted again. The judge was making a point, he was sure, but damned if he knew what it was.

The judge grunted his way out of the chair and worked his temples with his pudgy pink fingers. He turned back to his marshal and said, 'Rip, by God, I guess I have to spell it out, don't I?'

Rip knew he might not be the sharpest knife in the rack but he wasn't about to put up with that down-your-nose attitude by anyone, not even the judge.

'Judge, I've learned a thing or two these past few years as marshal of

Cayuse Falls and one of them is that shutting up and listening will get me further along the trail than if I was to talk all over someone who's already doing a good job of it.'

The fat man nodded. 'Right. I expect you know what I'm about to say. But I'll humor you. I need you to ride on out and intercept Mason well before he gets here. But well within my jurisdiction.'

'I'm a marshal, Judge. A town marshal. Your jurisdiction might be for a good chunk of this territory but mine ain't. Legally I ain't got the right to go but shy of a mile beyond the edge of Main Street, you know that.'

Pontiff sighed and said in a quieter voice, 'Rip, I'm sorry. I'm not making myself plain enough. As the overseer of the law in this region I'm giving you the right as a lawman to meet the man. I'm extending your reach, so to speak.'

Rip leaned forward, his fingertips together. 'I suppose I could organize a posse, deputize a few folks. Calvin and

Russell would help out, I know. They're always game for a bit of adventure. Anything to get away from the ranch. We'd be sort of escorting him back to town anyway. Not like I have to place the man in cuffs, though from what I've heard he's a prickly pear. I'd feel better if I could disarm him.'

'You're getting closer to the bone of the matter, Rip, but you got to keep chewin'.'

'What do you mean?' Rip's hackles were still raised.

'You'll need to do this alone. And you'll need to bring him in,' the judge leaned forward and stared hard at Rip. 'But draped over his saddle.'

Rip crossed his arms and sat straighter.

'Dead, Rip. I want him dead.'

'Why can't I bring him in alive?'

'Because he's a notorious outlaw. A murderer, Rip. Why, he's murdered old folks, babies, women old and young. He's nothing but a vicious killer. Shoots 'em for fun, so I'm told.'

'I ain't heard half of that. But say you're right, Newie, you're still asking me to kill a man without dealing him a fair hand from the law. That's wrong. You're a judge, Newie. And besides, I thought we was friends.'

'We are, Rip. That's why I'm asking you to help me here.'

'There's a lot more to this than what's laid on the table. I could get killed, Newie, you ever thought of that? Course you have, you always think of every angle before you commit yourself to anything. 'Cept this time I'm the one being committed to the thing. And I don't like it, plain and simple. You're asking me to kill a man.'

'I'm asking you to kill a killer. It's your job.' Pontiff barked the words and slapped his palms on the chair's worn arm rests. His voice echoed in the room. He worked his way back behind his desk.

Rip slapped his hat against his thigh. 'My job is to protect people within the town limits of Cayuse Falls. There's a sheriff who's hired to patrol the area beyond the town's limits. Get him to do your dirty work.' Rip gripped his hat brim tight and strode to the door. He paused, his hand on the knob, and said, 'I won't kill for you, Newie. That's breaking the law and I won't do that for any man. I don't want any of the things that committing a crime will get me.'

Pontiff leaned on his desk, his fingertips spidered on the blotter. 'How about your wife, Rip,' he said in a low voice. 'You do that for her? Or maybe she doesn't mean that much to you. Your job? Your life here in Cayuse Falls? I don't want you to do this because of all I've done for you, Rip. Hell, giving a man his freedom is something one man should do for another. And I was only too glad to do it for you, Rip.'

'No, I want you to do this because Mason plain needs to be dead. He's killed countless dozens of innocent people over the years and he'll never change. He's headed this way and if he's not stopped before he gets here, then he'll likely make his way straight through this town and kill everyone we hold dear.'

'Could you stand that, Rip, if your wife, God bless her, fell victim to such a scourge? Of course not. I don't want this sort of person running around loose in my jurisdiction, ruining the plans we have in place for this town. So far as I know I'm the only man, other than my contact in Kansas City, who knows Mason's heading to Cayuse Falls. And now you know, Rip.'

He stood and stared at the lawman. 'Return with Mason's body and there will be huge cause for celebration. You will never want for work again, Rip, being the hero who took down one of the West's biggest scourges, a man wanted for decades.'

The room was quiet. The last of the judge's words fading into the dark, oiled woodwork. Rip spoke. 'Why can't I bring him in alive?'

Pontiff slammed a hand flat against the leather desk blotter. The slap knocked a pipe from its rack and a silver letter opener clattered. 'Because I don't want him alive, dammit. I want him dead. And I'm the boss here.' Pontiff spit the words from his thick, purple face. 'I don't take questions, I give orders. If I can't have satisfaction from my most trusted employee, then I can damn well send his ass back to pounding rock and find someone else to deal with the one and only favor to date I've asked of him.'

Rip's jaw muscles tightened and he clenched his teeth so tight they hurt. He didn't care if his teeth snapped. It kept him from doing something he might regret. It took a lot to rile him, as the judge well knew, and he'd been well and truly riled.

Pontiff's face softened and he smiled. 'Hell, Rip, I've never asked you to do anything more than your job here in this town and you're making me sound like I'm giving ultimatums when all I really want is to make sure my town's protected, my people are safe, and my friend is afforded the title of hero for bringing in a notorious outlaw. You do that, Rip, and being marshal of this one-horse poke is only the beginning. I know your wife's been hankering after land of her own. Show up her daddy a bit. How 'bout a whole ranch, Rip? Hell, with a national hero for a husband, why Sue could have her pick of any amount of acreage from here to old Mexico. Make that old man's spread look like a play area for kiddies.'

One corner of Rip's mouth rose in a mock smile. 'And what are you getting out of this, Newie? Bound to be more than glory. That ain't enough for you.'

There was a flash of surprise before Pontiff grinned and wagged a finger. 'You know me too well, Rip. Too well. But you're right. My reelection would pretty much be guaranteed should a certain notorious outlaw meet his end in my jurisdiction. And it goes without saying, though I'm going to say it anyway, Rip, that it won't hurt my marshal none, either.'

'Don't you ever get dizzy talking in circles like you do, Newie?'

Pontiff's smile dissipated from his pudgy face and he said, 'Think about it, Rip. I got too much to lose and I know too damn much about a select few folks to go down empty-handed and alone. Think about it, Rip. Think long and hard on it.'

Rip didn't look at the judge. He knew if he did he'd walk back across the length of the fancy office and pile a fist right into that fat face. A face he didn't recognize anymore. Hell, maybe he'd never really known him.

McCorkle held his position at the doorknob for a moment longer. Pontiff said, 'That will be all, Marshal.' McCorkle pulled open the door and yanked it hard behind himself.

The slam rattled the two framed documents to the right of the door. One fell face forward, slipped off the book-case, and dropped upright to the floor. The process took so long that Pontiff watched the entire thing as if in a dream. Finally the framed document, his citation from Washington charging him with maintaining and enforcing the laws of the United States of America in this region, tipped forward, and came to rest, glass up. It was signed by the president of the nation and notarized by a secretary of something or other. And the glass, by God, did not break.

'Lucky,' said Pontiff. He stared at the square of glass for a long time. Then, as if awakening, he secured the curled arms of his eyeglasses behind his ears and set to work on a fresh stack of papers that needed his attention.

5

Rip walked slowly toward home and lunch with his wife. It suited him well enough, truth be told, to have this chance to own land on his own terms. Rip would finally be beholden to no man. But would he really? His pace slackened as he thought back on the exchange he'd had in the judge's office. Beholden to no man except the judge.

Bought and paid for, he thought. *That's me, a kept man.* No doubt he owed everything to Newie. Hell, he owed him his life, if he wanted to be honest with himself. That hurt, but it was the plain truth of the matter. Without the judge's letter sent all the way down to Exeter Prison, he doubted he'd even be alive today. Three years ago he'd sent for him.

And whatever he put in that letter was sure powerful stuff, especially considering that he, Ripley McCorkle, was a deputy marshal convicted of killing a muleskinner who'd been dealing rough play to that girl he'd dragged along with him into Rip's town. Come to find out it had been the muleskinner's own daughter, but not a soul in that town would stick up for Rip. That lawyer had somehow twisted a straight-ahead situation into something so coiled and dicey Rip still didn't know what happened at the trial. It finally sunk in when the judge whacked that gavel down and gave him thirty years' labor for murder. Thirty years for doing his job, for killing a raping rogue. Rip gritted his teeth as he walked.

He still wasn't sure what Newie was supposed to have done to land him in the hoosegow, but Newie had maintained his innocence for five years until he left. And he told Rip in a low voice, away from Jug, not that it would have mattered, that he'd get him out of there. It might take a while, but to have faith.

Then Newie had patted him on the back, shook his hand with a firm grip, and looked him in the eye, smiling as they led him away. And Rip had waited for three more years, his faith in Newie not faltering much, such was the man's ability to affect those around him with his positive demeanor. And besides, he had little else to look forward to.

And now here he was, marshal of a modest but prosperous town in a growing Western territory, and at a salary of twenty-two dollars a month that was slowly building up in the bank. He had married the daughter of a successful, if surly, rancher. And the only man in town who knew of Rip's convict past was the judge.

If he believed the judge then this little town was going to be one of the more important centers in this part of the West. Newie had him there, he'd given Rip little reason to doubt him in all the years he'd known him. Maybe he really could pull off the railroad deal. But to gun a man down without cause. That was asking too much.

He swung open the kitchen door and there was his Sue, a tall woman, the cuffs of her sleeves flopping above hands working deep in her yellow bread bowl, an ancient, chipped thing that had been her mother's. All of his walking woes evaporated at the sight of her, the light of the sun in her hair, strands hanging loose from the clip she wore. She was a picture.

'How's my Sue?' he said, leaning in and smiling.

She didn't turn around, but said, 'Good, you're finally home. Come here and pull these cuffs up, will you? I'm about to knead them into my dough.'

He hurried over and pinched the narrow white cuffs, trying to inch them up her thin arms to her elbows.

'Never mind. You are useless as tits on a bull, I swear.' He'd been ready to kiss her on the neck but he pulled back and stared at her bony, moving shoulders. After a few quiet moments she looked at him and said, 'What are you doing? Wash yourself. I'll have your meal laid out soon enough.'

He should have stayed at the jail. He had plenty to do and he wasn't that hungry anyway. If he wanted to be cursed at he would have stayed at Newie's. He should tell her that, he thought, as he went back outside to the porch. He washed at the pump by the steps and when he came back in, she said, 'You talk to Newie about your pay like we said you was going to?'

It annoyed him that she referred to Newie by that name. True, it was the judge's name, but she didn't know him like he did. She didn't know that he didn't like for people, apparently even Rip, to call him by that name anymore. Rip decided that she held the judge in too high a regard.

'You ought not to call him that,' he said.

'It's his name, isn't it?'

'Yes, but he doesn't like it. I don't even call him that no more.'

She stopped ladling dumplings into

63

his bowl and said, 'For heaven's sake, why not? And you his oldest, dearest friend.'

Rip ran a hand across his raspy face. Have to shave clean again tonight. Another of the judge's requests: *Only heathens sport stubble.*

'That's the way he wants it, Sue. With the railroad deal and the elections coming up I guess he figures the more professional he is from all angles, the less trouble he'll have.'

'Oh, please. That's got nothing to do with it. He's getting too big for his britches.'

This surprised him. He would never get a fix on this woman, he was sure of it.

She snorted and smiled, 'And that's the truth of it. He's filled out some. We know it isn't from my cooking. He ain't been here to break bread with us in more than a year.'

'I know. But it's the election. He's got a lot on his mind.'

'A lot on his plate, you mean.' She

snorted again and clunked the pan back onto the stovetop. 'What about your pay?'

'Sue, it's not the time for that, I told you. There are things going on that are more important.' He'd almost managed to forget about Mason for the time being.

'Ripley McCorkle, what's more important than our future? Do you want to live here in this little shack all your married life?'

He smiled. 'It's hardly a shack, Sue.' This was not shaping up to be one of her soft days. She was in a mood for a tongue fight and he had enough of that all morning with the judge. Still, if he did deal with Mason, he could give her the home she wanted.

He ate his stew in silence, blowing on the steaming chunks of soft meat and carrots and thick gravy, parceling out the dumplings so they lasted as long as the stew itself. She could cook, he'd give her that, too. He'd never want for a decent meal in her kitchen. He looked up at her, his admiration renewed with each bite.

She'd resumed her bread-making and he saw the firm outlines of her back and shoulder muscles moving this way, then that, through the blue flowered dress as she worked the dough.

'You do anything interesting this morning?' he said, knowing almost to a word her response.

'Does it look like it?' she said, not stopping the alternating arm motions. He listened to the steady clunk, clunk, clunk of the bowl on the countertop. Then she turned and frowned at him, picking bits of floury dough off her fingers. 'What's so important, Rip? What's he got you doing?' She stared at him a moment and he looked down at his bowl, took a big mouthful, and gulped from his glass of water. She turned back to working her dough.

He resumed eating, trying to avoid scraping his spoon against the bowl so she might not ask any more questions. He didn't have any answers anyway.

6

'I told you we should have gone around this damn rock knob.'

'You didn't tell me nothing. Except how tired you are.'

Other than their shared skill in forcing blushes from hardened men with language that came from living a rough-and-tumble existence, Belle-Ruth and Cheery Girl appeared, to strangers, as strangers to each other. In fact they were sisters of a sort, sharing a father, also the man responsible for their inventive vocabulary and, unfortunately for her, the one responsible for Cheery Girl's rather powerful appearance.

Belle-Ruth's pleasing features, smooth skin, and straight, blonde hair were the only gifts her mother, their father's second and final legal wife, bequeathed to her before she died of complications arising from her first waking view of the sheer enormity facing her of a lifetime of misery, raising not only her own fair baby but the large and overbearing presence of Cheery Girl, brought to their union by the man who had put her in this situation.

Nearly two decades later the young ladies, mere months apart in age but a world apart in appearance, took to the trail to escape blame in their father's untimely demise. They had thus far in their seven months on the trail managed to figure out, through a series of unintentional encounters with less-than-savory woodsmen and one confusing weekend at a mountain men's rendezvous, how to get along on the trail without actually having to work for a living.

Usually it involved a series of coercions from the seemingly helpless Belle-Ruth who somehow had managed to injure herself while bathing in a mountain stream or required assistance changing her clothes in the middle of a green meadow. And while her unfortunate rescuer attempted to suggest payment for help rendered, a grizzly in the form of Cheery Girl rolled through the brush and counter-offered with a few well-placed rounds from a Remington .44 — Cheery Girl was a crack shot, to her mind this skill was the only thing of worth her father gave her. And since Belle-Ruth was not capable of hitting anything but sky or dirt whenever she pulled a pistol's trigger, she stuck with her strengths, namely those already mentioned.

The young ladies always left their victims full of regret and empty of worldly possessions. No one as yet had caught them, there being few men who would admit to the situations in which they found themselves immediately following the one-sided and embarrassing gunplay.

* * *

Belle-Ruth squinted at her big sister, six months older and one-hundred pounds heavier, and said nothing.

'Oh, quit scowling,' said Cheery. 'You forget I'm a woman, too. And your sister. Ain't none of your womanly ways is going to work on me.'

They rode together in silence for another few minutes, and Belle-Ruth said, 'I'm hungry. You said we could stop for the night. And it's your turn to drag this dang mule.'

Cheery Girl looked pained as she reached over and yanked the lead rope from Belle's hand. 'Ow, hey!'

But Cheery Girl had stopped her horse and was stretching her head high, her nose in the air, working, as she dallied the mule's lead around her saddle horn.

'What's your problem?'

'Shut your whining mouth, will you?' Cheery said through clenched teeth. She motioned with her chin upwind toward the copse visible beyond the gentle rise ahead. 'Somebody down there.'

Belle leaned to her right. 'I don't see nothin',' she whispered.

'Neither do I,' said Cheery, 'but I can smell right enough.' She dismounted, pleased that though she was a big girl she was, in fact, light on her feet. She might never look like her sister but she moved like an Indian. And that was good enough, most of the time. She handed her reins to Belle and slipped her rifle from its sheath on her brown mare, Trixie.

They had done this so many times Belle knew to keep her mouth shut and trust Cheery's impressive nose. Belle sat straighter and closed her eyes, flexing her nostrils and sniffing long and loud.

'What are you doing?'

Belle opened her eyes. Cheery was staring at her. 'I'm trying to smell beef smoke.'

Cheery poked her. 'What if they're having bird?' She tramped off toward the stand of forest below them. Belle watched her big sister disappear into the trees, then she closed her eyes and inhaled deeply through her nose. 'It's beef all right.'

★ ★ ★

'A big 'un, older looking.'

'What's he doing?' said Belle, looking at the tree tops.

'Just feeding his fire. Got coffee on, though. And a fine looking stallion.'

'Cheery, we don't need another horse.'

'Well, we can't leave it with him. He'd get free and ride off, get the law on us. You want that?'

Belle shook her head.

'What's the matter?' said Cheery, staring at her little sister.

'Nothing.'

Cheery narrowed her eyes and leaned forward. She put a meaty palm to Belle's forehead but the pale girl pulled away. 'You sick?'

'Nope.'

'Then what?'

Belle shook her head again.

'It's that little drummer again, ain't it?' Cheery leaned back, secure in the knowledge that their whispering wouldn't carry upwind to the trees sheltering the big man.

Belle turned to face her sister and said, 'It's just that we ain't never left no one with nothing so far from a town before. He'll likely die out there.'

'He's a man, ain't he?'

'Yeah,' said Belle, flicking her horse's mane with a slender finger.

'Well, he deserves what he got then.'

Belle said nothing, but bit her bottom lip, her eyes nearly shut.

'Belle-Ruth, you ain't sweet on that little Irish fella, are you?'

Belle said something low, not looking up.

'What? Did you say something, missy?' said Cheery, her voice rising louder than she intended. But dammit she was mad. Listen to this ungrateful girl who would have starved to death — or worse, been the plaything of every damned man in creation — had Cheery not taken control of their lives.

'I'm sick of you bossin' me around, you hear? You're only older by half a year.' Tears trailed through the dust on Belle's pretty face.

Cheery half-smiled and tilted her head. 'There's more'n one way of being older, Belle.'

Belle wiped her eyes with the back of her hands and said, 'Can't we leave this one be?' A hopeful look raised her blonde eyebrows.

'Nope,' said Cheery. 'A man's a man.' She leaned closer. 'And besides, this one has the misfortune to look like Pa.'

Belle's features hardened and she looked ahead of them. 'All right, then. What are we waiting for?'

Cheery smiled and said, 'Let's go.'

★ ★ ★

Mason heard Bub nicker, but it was too late. He had enough time to swing to one knee, his left hand already dragging on his pistol, when through the stiffening wind he heard the throaty, dead clicking of a hammer eased back to the deadliest position of all.

'Aw, go on.' The voice was odd, too rounded for a man's. It came from a huge shape outlined against the pink and orange hues of a late afternoon Western sky. 'I got bullets.'

Mason, pivoting on his right knee, gritted his teeth and squinted from under his hat brim. 'Do I know you?'

The head of the big shape stared, then finally shook no, slowly.

'Ease that hogleg out slow, two fingers like you was pinchin' it, then toss it in the dirt toward me. Easy like, elsewise you might find yourself dead. That'd ruin a man's appetite for sure.'

Definitely a woman's voice. 'Now look, sister — '

From behind him he heard another series of deadly clicks. Surrounded by at least two. He did as the first commanded.

'You got it all wrong, bud. She's the sister.'

Mason shifted his eyes to the side but didn't turn around. He kept the big one in his sight as he eased the pistol from its holster.

'Take 'er easy, fella,' said the big one.

Never in nearly three decades on the trail had Mason had a more confusing and frustrating couple of days. He'd left his guard down far too long and he was paying for the error. He sighed, knowing he had earned, through negligence, whatever he was about to experience, though he still looked about himself, running through the available possibilities. There weren't many.

Bub was too far off, hobbled ten yards away. His saddle, gear, and carbine were flopped on the far side of the fire. His single revolver was in the dirt too far in front of him to help. And since there were two of them, one in front, one directly behind, any attempt to angle himself out of the sightline of the burly one would be tracked by whoever was back there.

'Belle,' said the big person, 'Check

him over. And no skimping. I don't want no surprise pistols nor knives.' He heard the crunch of dirt and twigs under boots then felt light hands try to push him roughly. He looked up and one of the prettiest girls he had ever seen in his life knocked the last pin out from under any possible plan for escape he may have cooked up.

She bent low over him and he saw right down her low-buttoned shirt. And while he was sure that was all part of the plan, he couldn't prevent his gaze from lingering there longer than he'd intended. He cut his stare upward and his eyes met hers. She giggled, exposing fine, white teeth. She was young enough to be his granddaughter.

'You like what you see, old-timer?' Her voice was breathy, soft, and warm. Everything the big girl's wasn't. 'You got pretty blue eyes, for an old-timer.' She giggled.

He didn't respond, save for his jaw muscle pulsing as he ground his teeth together.

'Let's go, Belle. This ain't no Sunday social.'

The blonde found his skinning knife and slipped it from its sheath on his belt, then patted him on the fleshy side of his belly, and giggled again. She backed away, still smiling at him, picked up the pistol, and tucked it into her own gunbelt, along with the knife.

She stood off to the side, her arms folded in front of her chest. All part of the plan, he thought. The big talker moved closer. Big, but definitely not a man.

'Now,' she said, wagging her pistol, 'take 'em off.'

He stared at her. Surely she didn't mean . . . and then the little naked Irishman came to mind. Oh no. No way. Mason, he told himself, how did you get caught like this?

'You heard me, old man. Strip down. Right down, boy, to nothin'.'

'Like hell.'

The two women looked at each other, then back to him. Did the big one hint that they were sisters? He didn't see it, but then again nothing should surprise him anymore. Maybe he was an old man, too stupid to keep his guard up, even for a few last days. I deserve this, he thought.

'Mister,' said the big one, raising the pistol and walking toward him, 'you take them clothes off or you're going to die where you kneel. Right there in the dirt.'

'Then shoot me.' He stared into her face, which he saw clearly for the first time. She was a dozen feet from him. There was no craziness there like so many trigger hounds seem to wear, but neither was there any fear. In fact, he swore she was close to smirking. A damn smug she-bear. She might shoot him.

'Belle, draw your gun. Aim it at the man. If he happens to twitch, shoot him.'

Mason watched Belle's face. There was a moment of uncertainty there and he bet she was no gunhand. The big one, yes, she would be a decent shot. And probably had the guts — plenty of those — to shoot a man. But they hadn't shot the Irishman. All they wanted was to steal items of worth, things they could sell, and devil may care what happened to their victims.

He'd keep his eyes on Belle. She was the weak link in this short chain.

The big one walked forward, skirted him. Her trousers and boots were in good condition, he noted. Not wanting for money. Further proof that they were good at what they did, if he needed further proof. He followed her with his eyes as she walked slowly around him, then cut his gaze back to Belle, whose pistol was held steady on him, though not with the confidence the big girl enjoyed. He didn't think she'd shoot him, too nervous. At least not for a slight movement of his head.

He followed the big one around as she walked behind him. As he figured, she was going to club him with the butt of her pistol, held like a hammer. Here she comes, he thought. He also thought that they should have tied him. She stepped in, her arm held high for the swing, and as it came down he spun, tensing his left foot under him, and reached up for her arm.

It was fleshy and muscled, all at once, but plenty to grab. He gripped hard and pulled her down on him, rolling onto his back as he yanked on her. She was a big girl, probably weighing in at close to his weight, though he had a good five, six inches of height on her. She slammed down on her back beyond where he knelt.

As he rolled his hat clopped off and landed in the fire. He felt the back of his head graze one of the rocks he'd arranged for a fire ring. The scent of cooked rabbit filled his nostrils.

As the big girl crashed down, he heard the pretty one scream. He held onto the fat arm, still by the wrist, and as the girl rolled with the momentum her big body had caused, he felt the bone pop under his palm and knew she'd broken something. The hand opened and the pistol dropped. He grabbed at it, and barely got it out from under her before her wide rump settled back down at his feet.

He was an eye-blink quicker than the little blonde girl and he backed away from them both. The blonde girl saw the futility of keeping her pistol aimed at him and tossed it to the ground. She dropped to her knees at the big girl's side, cooing and crying. He kept the pistol trained on the big girl, who was grunting her way into an upright position and moaning. She put no weight on the swelling wrist and swung it up to cradle in her lap.

'You son of a bitch,' she said, her voice low like a man's but quavering in anger and pain. He almost felt the hatred from her eyes as it reached him across the smoking fire. He held the pistol on her and nodded slowly as he bent to retrieve his hat. He waved it to clear any embers, held it against his belly and patted it with the same hand.

No hot spots, though there was a charred hole where none existed before. He stuffed it on his head.

In the commotion Bub had crow-hopped free of the camp and ended up in a tangle of hobble line and rabbit brush twenty yards off. He stood still but with nostrils extended and ears perked. Mason was sure the big black horse was watching him, eyes narrowed enough to let Mason know he was displeased. Bub did not like surprises and he'd had plenty in the past couple of days. Any more of this, thought Mason, and I'll be walking. Mason figured they had their own horses tied out of sight downwind.

The petite blonde girl made enough noise for the two of them. A stranger would be hard-pressed to know which of the two was injured.

'That's enough bawlin', Belle-Ruth. I don't need to hear it. Next time I tell you to shoot someone if they so much as twitch, by God you do it. You hear me?'

'You blamin' me?' said the blonde girl. Her eyes narrowed and glittered. She sniffed and leaned back as if she had been slapped.

Even if they don't look alike, thought Mason, at least they share a prickly demeanor.

'Enough,' he said.

They both looked at him. And he received pure hate from two sets of eyes. 'Save the anger. You attacked me, remember?' They stared at him as if he hadn't spoken. 'Get up,' he said, wagging the pistol at them. 'Now.'

They finally complied, the big girl shrugging off the support her little sister offered. They both glared at each other and at him, alternately. Great, thought Mason. We're all angry with each other.

'You,' he pointed the pistol at the blonde. 'Pull one of those joints of rope from your pocket. I expect they were for me. Well, now they're for you two.' He nodded at the big girl and said, 'Tie her up.'

The blonde didn't move. Mason shot the heel of her boot and she screamed. The big girl barely flinched. 'Tie her arms behind her back. Now.'

'But one of them's broke.'

'I know.'

'But —'

'Tie her. And tight.'

The big one glared at him. He ignored her. 'I said tight.' The blonde girl paused, chewed on her bottom lip, and pulled on the two ends of rope. The big girl sucked air in through her clenched teeth and her face lost what little redness was left there. The blonde whimpered and tears leaked from her eye corners.

'Now, step away from her and get your hands behind yourself.'

She did as told and he pulled the last length of hemp rope from her pocket.

'Spin on him! Do something, Belle!' said the big girl. But the crying girl looked down and held her hands rigid behind her.

He had a loop on one wrist. It

amazed him that such a pretty little thing was so hard-hearted as to ride with the big she-bull over there. He took his time, wanting the knots to be good and tight until he could set down the pistol and retie them properly. Behind him he heard a sudden, loud, coughing shriek from none of them. It was joined by a close crashing sound.

Mason barely had time to turn his head toward the noise before he was hit from behind. His body was pushed forward, the pistol cracked off a round, and his head snapped backward. Something large and warm slammed into his left side and his hat flew off. He hit the ground, his hands unable to block the fall. His forehead met with something hard and cold and unmoving.

★ ★ ★

The first thing Mason heard as he came to was a husky voice saying, 'He's about my size and I'm gonna take what I

want. I earned it. Now pull, dammit.'
Then he felt a tremendous pressure on
his chest, ease off, then pressure, ease
off, then more pressure. Something
partially covered his face and he found
it difficult to breathe. He worked to
open his eyes, but all he saw was
stretched brown fabric.

'You got the ropes good and tight?
He's a big'un, for sure.' It was the large
girl, he remembered. What happened?
He had turned the table on the girls but
somehow he was their prisoner again.
But how? He thought that the best
course of action might be to feign
injury or unconsciousness, they might
continue talking in his presence. But he
couldn't. The big girl was on top of
him, pinning his chest and making
it difficult for him to breathe. Soon it
became unbearable. He struggled and
kicked, tried to move his arms but they,
like his ankles, were tied.

'He's awake. Good.' The big girl
grunted and rolled off him, right over
his face. It felt as though a huge sack of

wet river sand was crushing him. She was off and behind him, and he blinked and gasped, filling his lungs with great gulps. *I feel like a landed fish*, he thought, as his breathing steadied. He blinked and looked up. The big one stared down at him, smiling. No trace of her anger was left on her face. She laughed. It sounded like a crazy man's laughter. Another voice joined in, higher-pitched and softer. He looked to his right and there was the prettier girl, looking down at him, too.

'What happened?' he managed, licking his lips and looking around. He couldn't move his arms. They were tied to his sides, that much he felt. He raised his head and looked down at himself. Expecting to see his ankles bound as well. But all he saw was his naked body stretched out before him.

'Still pretty fit for a grampy,' said the big one and laughed her man-laugh again.

'Give me my clothes, dammit.'

The big girl leaned close to within

inches of his face and said, in a low, slow voice, 'Like hell.'

He earned it, he figured. He lowered his head back to the ground, closed his eyes, and said, 'What's next? Get me drunk and tie me to a log?'

There was a moment of quiet and then he heard them both cackle as if indeed they had spent the afternoon drinking. He opened his eyes and the big one said, 'If you know about that then it won't come as no surprise when I tell you that you were knocked down by a big, dumb mule.'

Florence, he thought. *If I ever see that Irishman again . . .*

The blonde said, 'I told you it'd be worth bringing along.'

'Yeah, well, luck don't come in pairs but for those who make it.'

The blonde watched the big girl walk away, then she looked back down at Mason's face and smiled. She broke her gaze from his face and let her eyes slowly travel down his body. She stopped, looked back up at him, and trailed down some more. He closed his eyes and thought of how he might get down out of the hills and to Cayuse Falls alive. *If I could get free long enough to kill that damned Irishman's mule. Nothing good has happened to me since I came across that little foolish drunk.*

He heard a scuffing noise to his left and opened his eyes in time to see a filthy rag, wet and clutched in the fat pink hand of the big girl. He turned his face away but it was no use, she clamped that thing on his mouth and nose and he felt her weight on his chest again, holding him down. The stink was at once perfumed and disgusting, like sweet rank meat. He heard her giggling, a high, fruity sound, not at all suited to her size. He felt her chest on top of him wiggle with laughter. Then, despite his struggles, he felt himself losing consciousness. His last thoughts were of the little Irishman and his tinctures. *Powerful stuff*, he thought, *to have landed me here. If I ever see him again I'll* . . .

7

His first thought was of rain. Hard, pelting drops of the storm in his dreams. Before he was fully awake he heard the clattering storm hitting his windows with enough force to pull him from sleep. And then he awakened, safe and snug, in the downstairs bedroom of his newly built house at the east end of Main Street.

He listened to the rain smack the roof, the clapboard siding, the glass windowpanes, his eyes wide in the dark. Something to his left, toward the door, felt wrong, smelled wrong. The room was filled with a wet, clinging odor, leather and sweat and smoke and something more. Something angry. Could a man smell anger? He didn't know. But he suspected, since he was having such absurd thoughts, that he must still be asleep. He hoped he was.

His right hand lay close to his leg and he pinched his thigh. He sure felt awake.

His heart worked hard deep in his chest as if it were trying to get out. The smell was there, stronger than before. It was the outdoors in the room with him. The window was closed. All doors and windows were closed, he'd made sure of that before turning in. And yet there was the smell and his heart beating hard and his throat was dry. Unbidden, his head moved to his left, his eyes wide open, staring into the dark. Far off lightning pushed into the dark room and in the slash of light he saw a man sitting in the straight-back chair by the door, the chair on which Newie draped his clothes every evening.

Pontiff tried to speak but his mouth was too dry. He swallowed and tried again. In a whisper he said, 'Mason?'

There was a pause then the voice said, 'What makes you think I'd be Mason?'

It took Pontiff a second to place the

voice, then he knew. 'Rip?' He struggled upright in bed and stared at the spot in the dark where he had seen the outline of this trespasser. 'What are you doing in my house? In my bedroom? Why, it's . . . it's — '

'Late enough to be early. You feeling guilty already, Newie?'

'I don't know what you mean. I . . . I was dreaming. Are you drunk, Rip? This is breaking and entering here, Rip. I won't — '

'I'm not much drunk. What I am is angry, Newie. All this time you led me to believe that what was a helping hand was nothing but a way to call in favors now and again.'

'I can understand your hesitation to embrace the facts, Rip, but — '

'Newie, I've had about all the starched campaigning I can take from you for one day. Maybe for all time.'

Pontiff decided to keep quiet. He'd seen Rip angry a time or two dealing with rowdy ranch hands who had too much liquor and not enough sense to stay put when put there. They'd always regret making the marshal of Cayuse Falls angry. And after all, Rip didn't land in jail for being meek.

'I'll do it, Newie. For some of the reasons you mentioned, but mostly for my wife. Odds are I won't live through it, but something tells me if I don't do this you'll make my life worth less than spit, and I can't live like that here and I can't take my wife away from here, from her family. I'm stuck, Newie, which is where you wanted me anyway. So I need a few questions answered and then I'll leave you to it.'

Pontiff opened his mouth and shut it again. Protesting would be futile. Rip had already made up his mind and what's more he was right.

'How will I know this Mason? I looked but I don't have a poster on him.'

Pontiff licked his lips again and before he spoke, lightning, closer, filled the room with blue light. He looked right into Rip's eyes. He seemed closer to the edge of the bed, though still in the chair. How was that possible?

'He's a big, big man, older than me by a few years. Wears a single gun, but he's deadly. Must be grey-headed by now.' He paused, thinking. Then cleared his throat and continued, 'My contact person in Kansas City saw him but a month ago and said he was riding an enormous black stallion and wearing a tall hat and a black duster. Big fella, he's hard to miss. Oh, and blue eyes. He has cold blue eyes.'

'Sounds like you've got some personal experience with him.'

Pontiff closed his eyes and shook his head. 'No. Not me. Just telling what I heard.'

'Uh-huh. One more thing, Newie,' said Rip, rising, his slicker shining wet in the dark. 'I don't give a damn about the glory of bringing him in, Newie. Keep that all to yourself. And good riddance. What I'm interested in is money. Plain and simple. You want to treat this like a business deal between two strangers, then fine. I'll need enough to buy land — '

'I'll do you one better, Rip,' said Pontiff, pushing himself upright in bed. 'If you make this happen I'll set you up on the old Peterson place.'

There was no sound and Pontiff took this for a sign of puzzlement on Rip's part. He rushed to exploit the moment. 'Sure! Why, who do you think bought the lease out when they defaulted? Bank? Hah. I *am* the bank, Rip. Chairman of the board and all. Voted in last year. As they say in the South, we're in tall cotton, my friend.'

The marshal sighed quickly and spoke as if he'd been interrupted. 'Keep it. And you'll need to find yourself another marshal, Newie. After this, I'm through.'

Pontiff heard Rip's coat rustle, felt his boots clunk on the floor heading to the door. How had he not heard him come in?

'We'll talk about that, Rip.'

Rip paused in the doorway and said,

'You got something to say to me, Newie, say it now. 'Cause when I leave this room, our talkin' is through.'

Pontiff stared at the lighter color of the marshal's slicker in the dark. He didn't say a word.

★   ★   ★

He sat up in bed a long time after Rip left, listening to the rain, sure of only one thing — for the first time in a long time, he didn't know how things would turn out. He was unsure of himself. He didn't like the feeling one bit, and right now he wasn't sure what he might do about it.

Somewhere out there, walking around town in the rain, was the only man in the world who up until earlier today would have willingly called him a friend. And now that was gone forever. How many more eggs could he break before this cake got made?

8

Rip fished around on the closet's top shelf and pulled down his bedroll, canteen, and finally, from a nail, his long knife, hanging in its sheath.

'What are you doing?' Sue creaked the little door wider.

He hadn't heard her come up behind him. How in hell was he going to track a known outlaw, a killer of men, when he couldn't even hear his own wife creep up on him?

He didn't turn around. 'It's early. You should be in bed.' She didn't move, so he said, 'I shouldn't be gone too long, but I'd rather have it with me than not.'

'But where are you going?'

He knew he should tell her but he didn't feel like talking. Didn't feel like much of anything — he was plain tired. He walked through the kitchen, out the door, and flopped the gear onto the old sway-back table on the porch. They used to eat there of an evening in the warmer weather, commenting on how lucky they were to live in such a fine little house on the river, and in town, too. Those evenings were a hundred years off. He felt her eyes on him through the screen door at his back. 'I could use some coffee, Sue.'

There was a pause and then she said, 'OK, Rip. Give me a minute.'

It was still dark but he heard the rain slopping in that big puddle at the bottom of the steps. He took a deep breath and went back into the little kitchen. She was prodding the coals with a steel poker. Her face was tight, her jaws clenched. She's angry, he thought. This is not what he wanted. He'd wanted to be gone, lit out before she awoke. But he'd overslept. And he felt wet-eyed and hang-dog, like a case of the shivers was coming on. All that rain last night. His hat wasn't even dry yet. And his boots were still sopping inside. It'd take another day before they

99

were comfortable again.

He put a hand on her shoulder. She flinched, kept jabbing the coals, coaxing into place the two spruce chunks she'd dropped into the firebox. 'Sue, it's something I got to do. Shouldn't take no more than a day.'

She turned to face him. 'Town's your duty, not outside of it. What's Newie got you doing now?'

He gritted his teeth. He could lie. Dammit, was it that obvious that Newie told him what to do and when to do it?

'Is it why you were out late last night? Why you come back wet and smelling sour of whiskey?'

He nodded. 'I was walking around, trying to figure out a few things.'

'Rip, why don't you talk about such things with me? Not with some floozy and a bottle. I'm your wife.'

He backed away and pointed a finger right at her. 'There ain't never been no floozies and the bottle was two drinks at Sully's. I told you, I spent the evening walking around. You know I have to do

100

that. It's my job.'

'Leaving town ain't your job.'

He pulled an empty flour sack from the folded stack on the pantry shelf. 'I'll need a few things. Food, some coffee. Town'll reimburse us for provisions.'

She slid the sack from his hand and began filling it, slowly wrapping biscuits, the last of their wedge of cheese, sifting coffee into a smaller sack. 'So it is town business, then.'

He nodded.

She poured him a cup of coffee and handed it to him, looking at him for the first time in long minutes. 'Rip,' she put a hand to his forehead. Her voice softened. 'Your head's hot. You're catching a chill. You should be in bed today and nowhere else.'

He shook his head briskly and smiled, gulping the coffee. 'I'm fine, Sue.' His voice was hoarse. 'Nothing that won't work out of me in the sun on the trail.'

She wasn't convinced, he knew. She stared at him with her mouth set tight.

He leaned down, kissed her on the forehead, and scooped up the sack. From the doorway, he forced a smile, and said, 'Trust me this once, Sue. It's something I got to do. But when I'm back everything will have changed. For the better. Then we won't be beholden to nobody. Not Newie nor nobody. We'll show 'em all.'

He smiled again, a waste of effort, he knew. If she kept pressing him, all he'd want to do is curl up in their bed. It wouldn't take much to convince him, Newie be damned. But that would ruin everything. Especially their one chance at real money. And that money meant security. And freedom from the Newland Pontiffs of the world.

'But for now, trust me, Sue. And don't you go asking Newie about this while I'm away.'

He clunked down off the porch, stepped square in the big puddle, and was gone. Sue stood at the screen door, framed in the dim light of the kitchen, a hand to her throat.

The sun hadn't gotten a leg up on Main Street yet and no one was out as Rip unlocked the jailhouse, stuffed cartridges into a saddlebag, grabbed the scatter-gun he normally used for imposing order on rare Saturday-night saloon crowds, and relocked the door. He stepped down off the boardwalk and walked up the quiet street toward Hap's Livery, where he intended to rent a hide and saddle.

Less than twenty minutes later he was out of town, mounted on a fine dun, and heading into the foothills to the east of Cayuse Falls. His headache grew worse with each step of the horse and he wished he was home in bed, Sue keeping the little house extra warm for him, bringing him chicken broth, sometimes touching his forehead, that worried look on her face.

He wished for anything but where he was. But anywhere? Not quite, Rip old boy. His thoughts turned to Exeter

Prison and he knew that was one place he had no interest in seeing again. He also knew that if he didn't follow through with Newie's task, Newie would damn sure follow through with his threat. He knew enough about the little fat man to know his threats bore teeth. And Rip either had to do his bidding or go back to jail.

He knew he wouldn't last long as a wanted man. Question was, would Newie last long in Cayuse Falls if Rip didn't come through for him? He coughed and spat up a hunk of something green that didn't look good. Rip heeled the horse into a trot and off the road, hoping to intercept Mason's path long before town and well into the hills.

★   ★   ★

Though it was only August, as he rode Rip bunched his wool coat tight in a gloved hand under his chin. He forced himself to think of anything other than his own misery. He hated being ill and on the rare occasion when he was stricken with a malady, it was usually a doozy that took the heat from his stove for a week or more. Just like his father, his mother used to say. Strong back, weak chest. In his mind he still heard her, saw her smile. Not so much the rest of her face anymore.

Other than prison, he couldn't recall a time in his life when he felt this low. His boss, a man he'd considered his friend, had blackmailed him, his wife was apparently unimpressed with him, his father-in-law thought he was a gold digger, he had the makings of a fine sickness percolating in his system, his horse would rather take on water and float away, and he was headed into the wilderness to gun down an outlaw who some folks considered to be one of the finest shots in the whole of the West.

The dun nickered under him. He opened his eyes and realized he'd drifted off. The horse's ears drooped straight out to the sides and he looked almost as miserable as Rip felt. The rain had increased and he was still skirting the edge of the deep forest. He fought a shiver that worked up from his belly to his shoulders and head, and he shook for a half-minute straight. When it passed his jaw ached from gritting his teeth.

He worked the horse left through scrubby alders and between twin aspens, and fought to suppress another racking cough as the sky darkened and the rain sluiced down on him. He was sure that no other person in the world was getting so severe a drenching at that particular moment.

He gave over to the shivering and sunk his heels into the rib barrel of the snorting dun. What he wouldn't give to be hugging a pot-belly stove about now, but he was miles from anywhere that had such a comfort. He pointed the dun into the deepest part of the forest ahead, direction be damned, and looked for a sheltering stand of pines, alders, anything. He realized he'd been foolish in not bringing a tarpaulin. Hell, for that matter he'd been foolish heading out at all. At this point, he was sure he'd be laid up in bed for a week or more by the time he made it back home.

Instead of stopping and building a fire, as was his intention, he drifted in and out of sleep. Each time he came around, the horse would have stopped. He knew he was delirious but somehow he couldn't bring himself to raise a leg, slip off the horse, and go through the required tasks of making camp. It couldn't be done. Even clucking and heeling the dun each time he awoke was a mighty effort.

His right hand was clamped permanently under his chin, the leather glove and wool collar of his coat one sodden lump. He was sure his boots were filled to the brim and running over with rainwater, and though they were deep in the trees gusts of biting wind sliced straight at them, hurling rain, twigs, and leaves so hard it felt like they were under constant assault of cannon fire.

The day grew darker as they trudged on. In moments of wakefulness he knew he was headed in roughly the direction he wanted. He guessed it to be mid-afternoon, though the dank and oppressive layer of clouds and steady drizzle kept the day feeling like a constant near-dark. Hours before he had given up wiping the water from his eyes, nose, mustache, and was sure the lower half of his face was covered with a slick layer of phlegm from his leaking nose.

He'd heard of people dying of a plain old cold and he'd always thought it was because they were weak people to begin with. He heard thunder again, rolling from far off. He waited, too tired to count the distance between boom and flash. Seconds later he felt his head bob forward and didn't care. The crack of striking lightning whipped him wide awake. The dun reared and whinnied. And in that instant he swore he heard another horse, like the echo of his own, far to his right and upwind.

The dun, as if in response, nickered and shook his head, stomping a front leg. He wanted to say, 'What is it, boy?' but all he managed was a grunt. He forced his eyelids open. At first he didn't hear or see anything. But he smelled . . . smoke? It was faint, then gone, nothing but rain and blown leaves in the near gloom. He blinked his eyes hard to squish the water from his lashes and peered out straight ahead. Nothing. He looked to his right and there was a flicker, gone. There, and gone again. And then he heard another horse.

A camp with a fire. It had to be. He wanted it to be. Nothing else right now would make sense but a campfire and warmth. Lightning struck again, close, with no thunderous warning. Not fair, he thought, squinting in the direction of the phantom light he had seen. Branches whipped and clawed at him, the horse skittered sideways and each time a sapling raked its side, belly, or neck, it thrashed the other way. He hadn't the strength to rein it in and all he saw when he opened his eyes and kept his head upright were more branches and more slicing rains.

And then he was there, he sensed it, in or very near to a camp. He heard horses and a mule's braying. But still he saw nothing but rain and darkness and clawing branches and a crack and flash and it was so near he smelled something burning, the stink of a mine after the smoke cleared from a one-stick charge.

The scene before him surprised him and dispensed with any residue of sickness that bogged him down. Time stilled, rain and wind continued, but he no longer heard them. His horse bucked and thrashed and somehow he stayed seated. Not twenty feet in front of him stood the man responsible for this mess, the man who caused Newie to send him out here, to risk everything and all. There was no mistaking it, bigger than big, black duster, tall hat, and wide of shoulder. It was Mason.

Mason the Mankiller.

Rip would end this all now. There would be no camp for him and he didn't care. He had found his man and he could end this. There was no doubt. No questioning the right and wrong of it. The task was at hand and he was an officer of the law, doing what needed to be done. Doing what was asked of him. The flashing continued, all around them. Mason was staring at him, arms upraised, coming at him at a walk.

Somehow that killer would know, would be coming to pull Rip off his mount and slice him through. That's what mankillers did. They sliced and gouged and kicked and played with their victims and then they shot them. Little better than the savages who roamed the edges and shadows of the West. Well, this was one killer who would not get the chance to kill again.

Rip bit hard on the inside of his cheek and yarned on the reins to keep the dun from thrashing. The big man was closing in on him. Rip grabbed at the gleaming wet stock of the shotgun in its boot at his left knee and drew it out. It was loaded and he cocked and leveled it at the dim outline of the man whose arms were still raised, still walking at him.

As Rip touched the twin triggers the big man paused, arms still held up as if to — Rip heard a woman's scream but he didn't care. The task was almost complete. He could go home and forget about this period of his life. Forget about this day and what he had been forced to do in order to keep the wolves in his life at bay.

His finger squeezed back and for the span of a clock's tick, they stared into each other's eyes. His eyes denied this fatal blow and begged forgiveness, and the other's questioned him and doomed him for all eternity.

The barrels' blasts, miniature lightning of their own, illumined the mankiller not five feet from him and the dun switched and swung and the killer's face was large and pink and surprised and it was not a man at all. He froze, the shotgun aimed where the shape had been, and stared.

It was a woman. Under the broad dripping brim of that hat was a large and terrified and shocked woman and his shells had caught her full in the chest, arms still up and coat wide like she was about to take flight. She whipped backward to the ground, arms still raised, and her mouth working like a fish's. In the close lightning flashes he saw blood fill that mouth and a great gout of it slid down her cheek.

Then the dun recoiled and bolted and the world intruded in full, whooshing back with all the sounds and smells of its terrible self. The first thing he heard was screaming. A young blonde woman was on her knees, bent low over the large woman he'd shot.

The rain again pelted him, the horse was nearly beyond control, and the blonde woman was screaming and pounding her fists on the large woman on the ground. Then the screaming woman looked up at him and he saw for the first time that she was pretty. Very pretty, but the ugliness of what she was enduring would mark her forever.

And then it occurred to him that there were other people, bound to be, who would be coming for him. Women never traveled alone. Perhaps they were with Mason. He felt ill again and then the woman was shouting at him with her terrible beautiful face. And under her face appeared a pistol and her hand shook. He was not ten feet away. He kicked at the dun to move, to run anywhere.

None of this made sense. None of it could be happening. Yesterday, he was fairly certain that he would see many sunrises and sunsets, and now someone was leveling a pistol at him. He prayed it was dark enough to obscure her vision. He cut the horse to the right and gave it heel. He still gripped the scatter-gun. And then he heard a popping sound and realized he hadn't gotten that far from the girl after all.

Another shot and the horse nearly bucked him off and kept grunting and panting and a sound deep in its throat grew louder and louder. Something pushed at him from behind but he kept to the saddle. Then more cracking sounds like half-green wood being pulled apart, reached him. It sounded like the world's loudest campfire, dry wood devoured by hot, hot flame.

They ran and ran and there was the girl's screaming behind him, in him. Then there was just rain and wind, and after a long time he slumped in the saddle and remembered no more.

9

Belle-Ruth stood, numb and uncaring, in the black rain. She had emptied her pistol at the man and his horse, not caring what she hit, knowing that, despite her poor gun skills, at that close range she was bound to hit something. Even the damned horse. If that horse belonged to the stranger who shot her sister full on with a scatter-gun, then it deserved to feel a bullet, too. She only hoped at least one of the bullets made its way into the man.

But the wind and rain and coming dark made it impossible for her to tell if he was still in the saddle or had toppled. Or even if he was coming back for her. She hoped he was.

All of this occurred to her in the time it took to draw in a breath and push it out again — something Cheery would do no more. She looked down at her sister as if seeing her there for the first time. Belle's breath left her as she tossed the gun aside, dropped to her knees, and put her face close to her sister's. 'Cheery! Cheery!' She held her face in her hands and bent close. She kissed her on the cheeks, the forehead, and repeated her name over and over. 'Cheery honey, Cheery, don't go don't be sick don't go . . . '

'You finally hit somethin'.' Cheery Girl lay there smiling, her head half-cradled in the bowl of the big hat she had so recently taken a liking to.

Belle-Ruth leaned over her sister, and the big girl opened her eyes wide. Smiling, she said, 'You got that damn man for me, Belle-Ruth.' Then she closed her eyes.

★　★　★

The rain had stopped and the next day had arrived by the time Belle-Ruth roused herself from huddling over her sister's pale body. Cold, bright light fingered its way through the haggard treetops and showed the girl what she faced.

The camp was more than a mess, it was a wreck. The canvas they had set up for protection from the weather hung in a massive white pine, streaked with rips and wrapped as if hugging the huge tree. Their gear lay in a sodden lump. The fire, built against that massive boulder, was nothing more than a damp black smudge on the earth.

She was surprised to see all four animals, the big man's black stallion, the white mule, her mare, Tiny, and Cheery's beloved brown mare, Trixie, all still picketed and staring at her. Occasionally one of them would twitch an ear. Even the mule was quiet. Normally at sunup and sundown, without fail, that thing had brayed and carried on so you'd think it was a rooster.

'The storm,' she said to them, as if that explained it all. And perhaps it did.

She rose from her knees and hesitated there, wavering on stiff legs. She didn't quite know what to do. At last, looking away, Belle slid the big hat down over Cheery's face, biting her lip and stifling tears that rolled anyway.

She moved forward, slow, from being in the one position for so long. Tending the animals brought a feeling of usefulness and offered distraction, no matter how slight. But when it came time to lay out their gear in the sun, she managed to separate a few top items before she dropped to her knees and shook her head, her blonde hair hanging in clumps like wet golden wool.

After a while she moved back to her sister's side and arranged the big coat she had taken from that grumpy fellow the day before so that it covered the matted, greasy mess that was Cheery's chest. Most of the blood had washed away in the rain. Her wounds were puckered holes in the cloth and skin that looked as if worms had augered themselves in and out. Then she laid the big girl's arms on her belly, the large, dimpled hands resting atop one another.

As she worked she spoke, almost in a whisper, to her dead sister. 'I told you to wear that wrist in a sling, didn't I? And now look, it's gone purple and black.' She sniffed and rasped her hand under her nose. 'You said you were worried that person might be in trouble. You said you were going to lead his horse into camp. You weren't even wearing your guns. Now Cheery, why would that man want to harm you? I don't understand it. Truly I don't.'

Then she stopped fussing and sat quietly beside Cheery, one hand laid on her big sister's stacked hands. And it was in that position that she was awakened hours later by the braying of the mule.

10

'Hey, hey big fella!'

Mason felt as though he were underwater, gurgling sounds whooshing and popping all around him. Light now. Bright light and the pain it brings to eyes long closed and to a head already thudding with cannon fire. Sounds, more distinct. Like voices. And someone patting him on the face. He tried to speak, tried to say, 'Stop it.' It didn't work. He finally forced an eye open. And what he saw cleared his head better than any bucket of water or cup of scalding coffee.

The little Irishman leaned over him, his face inches away. He patted Mason's cheeks and smiled. He leaned back and spoke over his shoulder to someone. 'Ah, now, will you look at that. There's himself, awake and all. Good on ye, mister.'

'Get the hell off me.'

'I thought you weren't coming back to us here in the land of the living. Not that there's much promise at present, I'll grant you. But still . . . '

'Get the hell off me. Now.'

'Especially considering all that rain we had last night. I was sorely tempted to turn you over so you wouldn't drown but, well, you're naked as a babe. It didn't seem right. Or possible.'

Mason drew in a lungful of air and bellowed his command again. The little man winced as if struck and scrambled backward off Mason.

'You're back to your old self, so I see. That's grand then.'

'Stop talking.' Mason's hands were no longer lashed about his waist, and his feet were free of the ropes the women had used to restrain him. He pushed himself to a sitting position but the sky and trees traded places and his eyes watered. He closed them and raised himself the rest of the way slowly, not opening his eyes until he was sure the natural world had regained its rightful place in front of him.

'I thought so,' said Irish.

Mason did not respond. He ran his hands up his face and through his bristly thatch of steel gray hair. Something plunked on the ground in front of him. He looked at it through his fingers — a small, empty green bottle. He knew he would get an explanation, and he didn't have to wait long.

'The Professor's Patent Restorative Elixir. 'A drop or two will do, will do.' Looks to me as if they spent the entire bottle on you. It's meant only for rousing the nearly dead. But it can have the opposite effect on a person, too.'

'You don't say.'

'Oh, yes.'

Mason didn't want to but he opened his eyes again. The little man was to his left, squatting on his haunches and squinting at Mason.

'What?' said Mason.

The Irishman shook his head. Behind

him Mason heard a muffled munching sound. The donkey. Perfect.

'Why didn't you tell me you'd been jumped by women?' said Mason, massaging his temples with his forefingers in slow circles.

The Irishman looked down at his hands. 'Would you have?'

Mason nodded and said, 'No.' He got slowly to his feet and swayed there, looking about the little clearing. 'Rain, you say.'

'Yes, rain. I came upon you in the rain, shortly before it got dark, as a matter of fact. I'm afraid I tried to cover you with branches but it made more of a mess than anything else. And dragging you under trees would have proved no better. Besides, you're rather a stout fellow.'

'Appreciate you untying me.' Mason rubbed his wrists and flexed his hands. Within minutes he began walking in the direction he knew lay Cayuse Falls. The little man and his donkey followed.

'So, what's your name?'

'Why?'

Irish stopped and looked at the big, naked man. 'I'd like to know why you're such a belligerent man. I didn't ask you anything of a secret or sensitive nature, I'm quite sure.'

Mason nodded and the hint of a smile played his mouth corners. 'Name's Mason.' He stuck out a mammoth paw and Irish looked at it, then smiled and yanked it like a pump handle.

'Good to meet you, Mister Mason.'

They walked a few paces, then Irish said, 'Just Mason?'

'Don't push it, Irish.'

The little man nodded and kept walking. Half an hour later, after seeing Irish stroke his chin and run his hand through his hair, and clear his throat for a good ten minutes, Mason said, 'Spit it out, Irish.'

'What's that?' said the little man, as if someone had awakened him.

'You're itching to fill the air around us with words, so have at it.'

'Well, sir. Now that you bring it up, I admit I'm curious to know what it is that you do? I've told you all about meself, but I've heard nary a word about you.'

'Why?'

'It's apparent that you're a man who is not too fond of the company of strangers. That I've already deduced. That you're — '

'I kill.'

'What?'

'You heard me.'

Irish swallowed audibly. 'What . . . is it you kill?'

'I kill killers.'

'What . . . you mean rogue animals?'

Mason forced a thin smile. 'Yeah, something like that.'

They walked together in silence for a few more steps, then Irish said, 'You don't mean bears and cougars and wolves and such, do you?'

'Would it help you sleep better if I said yes?'

Irish was quiet for a few more steps,

then he said, 'Yes, I believe it would.'

'And if I answer, will you shut your mouth?'

Irish nodded.

'Then the answer to your question is yes.'

Irish nodded and nothing more passed between them until it became too dark to see. They made a meager camp in near silence, each man lost in his own thoughts.

11

Calvin Stropworth, the younger of the twins by four minutes, stomped into his second boot and pulled on the patched coat he shared with his brother, Russell. Both arms were in the sleeves but the jacket flapped open. His low-crown hat rode far back on his head, and the dark curls that a few local ranch girls adored from a distance trailed from under the brim. The boy picked his way through six inches of runny mud between the house and the first barn.

The ranch was set deep enough in what their father named Stropworth Valley that the sun hadn't dragged itself up above the hills to the east limning the little cleft in the hills. There was enough light to guide the boy forward to the small side door of the stable. As soon as he opened it the close, stinging smells of a barn shut tight all night clouded his eyes and nose and he flung the door wide.

'Mister,' he said to the string of sullen faces staring at him through the dank gloom, 'I don't see why I have to do chores alone. Not like he amounted to anything last night — stayed up is all, waiting on a calf that from the looks of things never did show. But he gets to sleep in.' Calvin shook his head and toed a drowsy hen out of his path.

He swung open the big double-doors at the far end of the barn. They led on up to the lower pastures, where the sheep and young cattle spent their days grazing. The sun had risen enough to edge the hilltops with a glow, the mist swirled and rose from the soaked land as if steaming. He kicked the headsize gray rock that held the left door in place and looked again toward where the sun was busy poking its blazing head up over the hilltop. And there, skylined at the peak, was a riderless, saddled horse standing stock still.

Calvin saw regular clouds of steam rising into the air from the strange horse's nostrils. He squinted and leaned forward and swore he saw something hanging from the belly of the beast. Dip, the kid goat, and three pecking hens, scattered before him as he ran back through the stable. He reached the entry door and paused with a hand spread on the latch. No sign yet of his father or his brother. Not even a slip of smoke from the kitchen chimney. 'I'll tend to it myself, then. Probably a stray anyway.'

He returned to the double doors. The horse was still there, now with its head down. It was a good quarter mile to the top, Calvin knew, but something compelled him to run straight uphill and find out who the horse belonged to.

He was still far from the beast when it nickered and perked its ears at him. He slowed his run to a walk and saw there was indeed something hanging from the horse's belly — it was a man's leg still stirruped. The rest of the man was attached, flat on the ground in a dark, sodden crumple.

Calvin licked his lips and ran forward. As he approached, the horse nickered again and walked a few steps, dragging the form another foot or so. He looked back down the hill at the house and barns. Too far to yell. They'd never hear him. Besides, it'd probably spook the horse. He should have gone for help before coming up.

'Easy there. Whoa, boy.' He reached the horse's neck and patted, clucking and offering reassuring words, all the while walking back toward the body. A filthy rain slicker trailed behind the man like a woman's cape. He bent low over the stretched body and his eyes widened. He leaned closer. He was sure now. It was his sister's husband, Rip.

He knelt there in the mud and listened for a heartbeat. And he heard one. 'Rip! Rip, you all right? Talk to me, Rip.' He slapped the man's cheeks but there was no response. He didn't appear to be too worse for the wear. Maybe a broken foot, a sore head. He hoped that was all.

Probably fell out of the saddle, caught his foot in the stirrup, and hit his head. No matter, he thought as he worked to free Rip's foot from the stirrup. The ankle was too swollen, so he hacked the boot apart with his folding knife, careful to not nick the already discolored and inflamed ankle.

Calvin's hands shook as he worked. The horse's legs trembled and it flicked its ears and shook its head at him. He guessed it was tired and confused. 'OK, fella. You're going to have to help me. He's a skinny drink, but I can't heft him all that way on my own. That's what horses are for.'

The young man straddled his brother-in-law in the mud and grime, wiped more dirt from the unconscious man's face, and noticed the man's nose was packed with mud, too. 'God, Rip, you did a number on yourself.' He fished out what he could, making sure the man's mouth was clear. Then he checked the ragged breathing again and said, 'Let's go, Rip. Time to get you inside.'

He slipped his hands under the man's arms and lifted. He got him upright, the tall man flopped over Calvin's shoulder like an exhausted dancer. Calvin worked the man over toward the dun, but the horse shied, sidestepping in a clumsy way, and neighing. 'Easy, you dumb horse. I got to get your rider mounted, even if it's on his belly. Won't be going far, you'll see.'

He snatched the reins with a free hand and managed to get Rip leaned against the horse. Speaking easy he reached behind the flopping slicker and gripped a handful of Rip's trousers at the back. As he bent low to lift the man up onto the saddle, his face rubbed against the mud-smudged fabric. And it was then he noticed, up close, the ragged, crusted bullet holes in the coat.

He froze, not even daring to breathe.

Shot in the back. He looked again at Rip's belly and noted for the first time that there wasn't just mud there. Would all this jostling kill the man? He put his ear to Rip's shoulder, but heard only the breeze, the horse's nervous nickering, and his own stuttering breath. 'Rip, hang on. I hope this ain't gonna do you in, but we got to get you to the house.'

He hoisted the man onto the saddle and lashed an ankle to a wrist under the horse's belly in hopes of preventing Rip from slipping off the horse. The horse stepped and stopped, stepped and stopped. Calvin held the reins and walked wide to look at the horse. Sure enough, in the increasing light, he saw wounds on the horse's muddied flanks. So the horse took lead, too. The far back leg appeared to be uninjured, but the closer leg was swollen, bunched in fist-size knots in a couple of spots.

He coaxed the horse into a walk again, and after a few feet the dun's gait loosened enough to permit it to head downhill in switchback fashion.

Calvin's breathing had slowed and he fought back the urge to shout in full voice for help. It would do no good yet.

'Come on, boy. You can do it. You're almost to fresh hay and water. We'll get you fixed up in no time.' He looked quickly behind him up the hill, certain that whoever did this to Rip and the horse was behind him. He expected to hear the drumming of hoofs and see a dozen riders with blazing eyes crest the hill, rear up, then descend on him like turkey buzzards on a dead calf.

Soon, though it felt like years, they were close enough that Calvin thought he might rouse someone from the house. He squinted down at it and was relieved to see a budding wisp of smoke spiral from the kitchen chimney. That would be his father.

'Pa! Pa! Hey the house! Help! Hey, hey!' On and on he yelled, dragging on the reins and checking on Rip, before finally he saw a dark wedge widen at the kitchen's red door. He yelled louder and as he passed the corner of the barn his father stepped outside. At the same moment, the horse stopped short, shaking and wobbling as it tried to draw up its wounded rear leg.

Calvin untied the strip of rein he used to keep Rip on the saddle, and eased the tall man down to the ground. The horse sidestepped awkwardly away from them.

'Pa! Pa, come quick. It's Rip.'

His father was already halfway across the muddy yard pulling on his second boot and hopping in the mud. In seconds the tall, older man bent down by his son's side. The two stared at Rip. Skin Stropworth patted Rip on the face, grabbed the man's hand and rubbed it between his own large callous-hardened hands, and said, 'Tell me what's gone on here, boy,' turning his eyes on Calvin.

But his son, relieved of the burden, shook as tears built up in his young eyes. 'I killed him, Pa.'

'What?' said Skin, bending low and putting an ear to his son-in-law's chest.

'Calvin, he's still breathing. Son, what do you mean? You did this?'

The boy shook his head and wiped at his nose with the back of a muddy hand. 'No, I found him like this up on the hill yonder, but bringing him down here on horseback . . . it can't have been good for him.'

'Nonsense, son. How else you going to get him on down here.' Skin looked up. 'Was there any sign of your sister? Calvin, listen to me. Any sign at all?'

The boy looked at his father, at the simmering frenzy in his eyes.

'Was your sister up there, too?' The man nearly shouted.

'No, no. He was alone. Near as I could tell, anyway. We got to get him up, Pa. Off the dirt. He's been shot in the back.'

The old man's face paled. 'What?'

'Horse, too.' Calvin looked over at the dun, leaning against the steaming boards of the barn, its left rear haunch weeping blood in the raw morning light. The dun's head was dipped low and it panted, its sides working hard.

'We'll thank that horse later, if there is a later for Rip. Run ahead and get the door. I've got him.' Skin slipped an arm under Rip's knees and another up high under his back. He lifted him as easily as if he were carrying a new calf out of the brush and into clear pasture for its mother.

'And yell for your brother. He should be up, by God. Then put on some water to boil. We got to clean up Rip, see what we're facing.'

Calvin dashed to the house, banging the front door wide and yelling his brother's name. By the time Russell made it to the kitchen, Calvin had cleared the remainder of last night's evening meal off the old slab-pine table, and his father laid Rip there, head toward the cookstove. Calvin poked at the stove and jammed more chunks of wood into the firebox.

'He alive, Pa?' said Russell, his face white and his eyes wide as he slipped his suspenders over his shoulders.

'He's alive. Get your boots on and saddle Gray Ghost. You'll need to ride to town. Get Doc Schmidt first thing, then to your sister's. Be calm about it. Tell her Rip's been hurt, he showed up at our place, and we need her here. Don't be making up things that will only worry her. Doc'll have his own horse, so send your sister on Gray Ghost and rent a horse from Hap's for yourself.'

The big man reached behind him and lifted the lid from a bean pot. He rummaged inside, tossed a small buckskin sack to his son, and said, 'Get Doc here first. Don't wait for him. Tell him it's bad. Don't leave the livery without paying. Mind you, only pay what's fair. Go now. And don't spare the horse. He can take it.'

'But Pa,' said Russell in a small voice. 'Gray Ghost is your horse.'

'I know. That's why I'm sending you on him. He's the fastest we've got. Now go!'

Russell and Calvin exchanged worried nods, then Russell snatched his hat from its peg before heading out the door.

'Calvin, dump some warm water in that pan and scare up some rags. We got to strip him down and wash him before we do anything. And while you're doing it, tell me everything that happened.'

As they eased the filthy clothes from the thin man, Calvin related to his father how he'd found Rip and the horse on the hill.

'So that's what happened to his boot. Bad as it is, that ankle's the least of his worries right now.'

They heard rapid hoofbeats squelch through the mud outdoors and knew Russell was on his way to town. 'More wood on that fire, boy. We got to keep him warm. Fetch quilts while I roll him onto his stomach.'

Calvin was back from the stove in seconds and they both stared at the three puckered wounds, two clustered up high on Rip's right side, one lower on the same side. Skin swallowed and said, 'That bottom one passed through.

But them others, they're still in there.'

'He gonna die, Pa?' said Calvin, staring down at his naked brother in-law stretched out on the kitchen table. He'd never seen a person so thin or so white.

'I honestly don't know, son. But it ain't good. He's a tough bird, but for all that, bullets are tougher.' He soaked another rag in the pan of water, now the color of swirling mud, and dabbed and stroked until the worst of the filth was cleaned away. 'Dump that water and get some fresh, boy. No one ever got clean by washing in muddy water.'

Skin wadded the rag around his smallest finger to clean close to the wounds. 'I warned your sister about marrying herself to a law man.' His voice was nearly a whisper. 'Now look what's happened. Lord, lord, but this is a dark day.'

They were quiet for a moment, and then Calvin said, 'Should we try to get them bullets out, Pa?'

Skin squinted in concentration at the

thin back of his son-in-law. 'No, Calvin. We'd better leave that to Doc. I reckon we'd do more harm than good were we to go digging in there. Might start him to bleeding again. And he's probably lost enough blood. Lord, but he's a pale one. Help me pack these quilts under him. I don't dare move him from the heat of the kitchen.'

Calvin kept the fire stoked until the firebox glowed like a ripe tomato. He went out twice to refill their wood supply from the shed at the rear of the house. He was dumping his last armload into the woodbox when his father whispered, 'Calvin, shush! He's coming around.'

And sure enough, the thin man's face, gaunt and whiter than any skin Calvin had ever seen, twitched with movement. The violet eyelids under the dark brows fluttered but didn't quite open. The nostrils at the end of the long, thin nose quivered above the matted moustache, and the chapped bottom lip worked up and down, almost twitching. A thin noise like steam rose from his mouth. Skin leaned close and said, 'Rip, son. It's all right. You're here at the ranch, Rip. Rest easy. Don't speak. Just rest.'

But the thin man, with only his bald head visible from beneath the heavy patchwork quilts, whispered, 'Newie, no, not Mason. He's a killer. Not right to ask of me, Newie. Kill Mason, it'll all be all right. Sue won't have no worries. Get our own place, show Skin a thing or two. Won't be beholden . . . '

Skin stood upright, his eyes wide, and stared at the twitching man. He looked briefly at Calvin, then back to Rip. He leaned down again and said in Rip's ear, 'Hush, Rip. Hush. You don't know what you're saying.'

He straightened again and said, 'Calvin, go out and get the barn chores done. I'll stay here with him. Put that horse inside, water and feed him up, and I'll see if we can't get Doc to dig those slugs out of his flank. He's a livery horse. Someone'll have to pay if he dies, and it won't be me.'

12

His bare feet kept Mason to a slow pace, and because Irish wore Mason's old socks, though they were wet and mostly worn through, he kept up with the big, silent man, but out of range of the branch Mason swung as he walked.

Miles back Irish had ripped apart the long underwear below the waist, enough to give Mason the lower half as a pair of makeshift pants, and he kept the upper half, which resembled a ragged night-shirt.

Mason tied a strand of hemp from Nubbin's lead rope about his waist, cinched it tight, and said, 'Thanks for the garment,' then moved off, swinging his staff and leaving Irish and the donkey both staring at his great naked back.

Hours later, Irish said, 'Why don't you like me, Mason?'

Just before a rough cairn of boulders at the edge of a thickly treed copse, Mason peered into the dense tree growth ahead. In a low voice, he said, 'Because I like myself just fine. And you're everything I'm not. Now get down.'

'But that's no — '

'I said to get down!' He growled. Mason grabbed Irish by the shoulder with one meaty paw and pulled him down to the ground. 'Shut your mouth and listen.'

Their faces werc inches apart and yet Mason wasn't looking anywhere but straight at the rock. A long, hollow moan, like wind through a mountain crevice, reached them. Irish's eyes widened and Mason squinted. A second sound, rasping and higher-pitched, joined the first, and they both squinted above the edge of the nearest boulder.

Mason knew he'd heard that noise before, but where? What terrible, painful sounds. They made the hair on his head prickle and itch.

'That's them! The ones who robbed me blind!'

'Don't you Irish ever speak in anything but a shout? And how do you know who it is?' said Mason.

Irish spoke again, this time in a whisper. 'Because that's my lovely Florence, the mule.'

Of course, the mule. The damnable mule.

'What do we do?' Irish twitched and fidgeted.

'What's this 'we' business? You have a mouse in your pocket?'

The Irishman looked up at him. 'I don't have any pockets.'

Mason sighed.

'Won't Nubbin be so pleased to see her again.' Irish leaned over and said in a whisper, 'They're what you might call a bit of an item, so they are.'

Mason looked down at the man as if he'd stepped in fresh dung. Then the little donkey brayed and lunged forward, whipping the rope from his master's hand. 'Nubbin!'

'Shush, they'll hear you,' said Mason, though he doubted whoever was in the camp could hear anything over their own noise.

Nubbin galloped straight into the thicket, braying enough to add a third element to the already awful racket.

Irish smiled wide eyed at Mason. 'You see? He's overjoyed.' He tried to stand, to join the party, and Mason yanked him back down. 'Keep quiet. They'll be back here, but if we keep low they'll think that big-eared rat followed of its own accord. Then we can get the drop on them.'

The low moaning stopped, as did the mule's braying. Only Nubbin's squeezebox sounds remained. He went on and on.

Mason retrieved his stick and said, 'You walk straight in, don't look around and give my location away. I'll work around the right side and take them by surprise.'

He looked at Irish and nodded. 'OK?'

Irish nodded and said, 'But how did they make it down here without us seeing any sign of them along the trail?'

'There's more than one way out of the mountains,' said Mason. 'But now I know exactly where we are. From here on there's only one route to Cayuse Falls. And we're on it.'

'And so, it appears, are they.'

'Yep. Let's go.'

Despite the little man's obvious desire to be reunited with his mule and donkey, Mason had to push Irish into the trees. When Irish turned around, Mason was gone. He couldn't even hear him. He took in a deep breath and pushed through the low, thick branches. Within seconds he heard a clicking like sticks snapping, and a voice said, 'Get outta there, damn you, and do it now!'

He wondered for a brief moment if perhaps she, for it was a woman's voice — the younger, pretty girl, if he wasn't mistaken — hadn't meant someone else. Perhaps she heard Mason instead. It would be foolish to move and potentially tip her off to his location. He froze. Almost. His right leg jumped and twitched on its own, rustling twigs and leaves. He couldn't stop it. And it didn't matter, for in the next instant the trunk of a thigh-size pine next to his head exploded.

He screamed and the shrill pitch of his voice surprised him. He felt hot needles of pain on his neck and face and he pitched forward out of the trees and into a clearing, landing on his face nearly underneath Florence the mule. She sidestepped and paddled the air with her back hoofs.

Irish heard the woman yell over his own cries for help. He looked up — he was pleased to note his eyes still worked, convinced seconds before that his sight had been robbed from him — and saw Mason behind the blonde girl, one thick arm under her throat, the other gripping the girl's wrist, racking it up and down in an effort to dislodge the pistol held tight there. The girl stood no chance against the big man and within seconds she had stopped struggling and sagged in his arms. He eased her to the ground and there she sat, her legs out in front of her, her head bent forward, her arms flopped on the grass at her sides.

'Good job, Irish, with all that caterwauling and carrying on. Gave me plenty to work with. I thought something really was wrong with you.' He laughed. The little man pushed to his feet and stood trembling beside the white mule, one hand resting on Nubbin's back.

'There is something wrong with me, man! I'm bleeding. I may actually die. Do you not see my wounds? I've been shot by this . . . this . . . criminal hussy!' He waved a bloody hand in their direction.

Mason and the girl exchanged glances.

'Huh,' said Mason. He motioned to the girl with his chin. 'Tend to him.' He cocked the pistol. 'Do it right, or there'll be hell to pay. And don't think I won't just because you're a woman.' He stepped backward. 'Apparently you're also a criminal hussy.' He shook his head and smiled. That Irish and his lingo.

The girl didn't move.

'Girly, didn't you hear me? You and me, we need to have ourselves a palaver. But first, let's get the little funny-talking fella over there tended to before he expires on us. What a shame that would be.' Still, she didn't move.

Mason looked at Irish and sighed. 'Wipe your face, then tie her up so she doesn't try anything stupid.'

Irish took a few faltering steps forward, convinced himself he could still support his weight and walk at the same time, and said, 'Well, what about the other girl, the big one.'

Mason motioned behind himself with the pistol. 'Dead.'

The blonde moaned low and loud. They both stared at her. So she was the source of the first sound they'd heard.

'Ah, the poor dear'll be in mourning,

no doubt.' Irish canted his head and looked at her, sympathy working his features like a mask.

'If they didn't go around jumping innocent folks and robbing them, maybe she'd still be alive.'

The girl spun around, rose to one knee, and said, 'Men? Innocent? What do you know about it? You don't know a damn thing!' She held her face in her hands, quiet, but her shoulders convulsed in silent spasms.

'You really should be more sensitive to other people's emotions, Mason.'

'Irish, keep it up and you'll be picking more than tree bark from your face. Besides, it wasn't my doing. I don't go around killing people.' He turned away. 'Least not without a damn good reason.'

Mason's eyes rested once again on the dead girl. She didn't seem nearly as bulky as she had the day before. He noticed his battered grey hat was pulled low over the girl's face. If he hadn't already reached down and touched the back of one purple-white hand resting on her stomach — dead a while, she was long cold and beginning to stiffen — he would swear she was sleeping. But he'd seen and heard the shot at Irish and he was convinced that no one could sleep through such a ruckus.

He also noticed that his black duster was drawn closed over her chest and stomach, the upper front chewed full of ragged finger-size holes — shotgun at close range. So she'd been wearing his coat when she was shot. Might mean something. Might mean nothing. Right now he needed a few answers. He reached down and plucked his hat from the girl's face. Her eyes were closed and she looked relaxed. Aside from her bluish pallor she might have been sleeping.

'Why, you can't wear that hat now, Mason,' said Irish. 'It's been adorning the dead.'

'Not all that much difference between alive and dead, Irish. Besides,' Mason turned to face the little man, winked, and tapped the brim. 'It's my best hat.'

He inspected the bindings Irish had put on the girl's wrists. They were loose and poorly knotted. 'Useless,' he muttered and retied them. The girl had lapsed back into her ragged, somber mood.

'Irish, make a fire . . . if you can. Then find some food. And for Pete's sake, put some clothes on. You look like a woman in that little dress. I'll be back.' Mason scanned the perimeter of the clearing, studying the ground, trailing off away from the camp, returning within minutes, and striking out again in a different direction. At last he walked back to the horses and patted the big black stallion on the neck. 'Bub, good to see you. Though why you would want to take up with the criminal element is beyond me.'

He noted the remnants of gathered food — leaves and bark littered the ground within reach of each horse. And a damp canvas bucket lay in the grass nearby. So the distraught girl at least had sense enough about her to tend to the beasts.

Mason was turning away from the horses when he saw the donkey at the end of the string. Nubbin stood tight to the mule, his head leaned against the larger animal's shoulder. The mule stood still and was quiet. 'Good job, Nubbin,' said Mason in a whisper.

★　★　★

'I didn't think you had it in you, Irish. But for beans and biscuits, this is pretty tasty.'

'I thank you for the compliment, but what makes you think you know a thing about me, Mister Mason?'

Mason spooned more beans onto his plate. 'You mean there's more to you than what you told me about your childhood, your cousins, your homeland, your poor sainted mother, your drunken uncles — '

'Leave him be.'

Irish and Mason looked at the girl.

155

She sat Indian-style at the edge of the fire, her hands tied in front of her so she could feed herself.

'Well, Irish. Looks to me like you have a champion.'

Irish said nothing, but Mason caught him staring at the girl over the rim of his cup. The little man sipped for a long time.

Mason tossed his tin plate and spoon on the ground beside him and licked bean drippings off his thumb, belched through closed lips, and pulled his makings from his vest pocket. He was pleased to note the big girl hadn't taken a liking to his vest, too, otherwise he'd have a smokeless meal, and that would be about the last straw. He torched it off, drew on it for a moment, then said, 'Sister, we need to talk. I've given you space and time, but you owe us some answers.'

'I don't owe you a damn thing.' She spat the words at him, low and snarling.

Mason drew on his quirley, then said, 'Did you get a look at whoever did that to your sister?' He kept his voice low and even, if not friendly.

She said nothing, just pulled her knees up to her chest and stared at the fire, the crackle of it the only sound in the near dark. Then Irish said, 'Only we're after making it right, you see.'

She turned to look at Irish and said, 'Making it right's my job, not yours. She was my sister.'

'Yeah, but she was wearing *my* clothes. That makes it *my* business.' Mason flicked the stub of cigarette into the flames and stared after it for long minutes.

'You're thinking that you were the target, then, Mister Mason?' said Irish, eyes wide.

'I am.'

'My sister was a good shot.'

'Not good enough.'

'I should kill you for that,' the girl said to the fire.

'Sister, I think you'd do well to leave off the renegade outlaw life you've been pursuing.'

'Why?' she said. The firelight reflected the glint of defiance in her eyes.

'Because I've seen you shoot.' Mason reached for the coffee pot. 'If you were any good, at that distance you should have killed him.' He gestured with the pot across the fire toward Irish.

'Now see here, Mason,' said Irish. 'I'll not take much more of this character abuse. For that's what it is, sure as there are stars in the heavens. Character abuse.'

'Could be a lot worse, little man. Think on that. And don't anybody try anything stupid tonight. I'm a light sleeper and this pistol has a hair trigger.' Mason smiled. 'You may have noticed that earlier, Irish. Back there in the trees?' Irish looked beyond the horses and mule and donkey into the dark, then back to the big man. Mason pulled his blanket over his shoulders and said, 'Now get some sleep.'

★ ★ ★

By the time Irish awoke the next morning, the fire had been rekindled, a pot of coffee was steaming on a rock close by the flames, the girl was sitting upright, as she had been when he went to sleep, and Mason was nowhere in sight. A glance behind told him that the man's big black horse was gone, too. Irish's two animals, plus the girls' two horses, were still picketed. He sat up and said, 'Good morning to you, ma'am.'

The girl looked at him. 'He's gone off, but he said he'd be back. You always sleep this late?'

'Gone? But he's coming back. Good, good.'

'You kept calling him 'Mason' yester-day.'

'Why yes.'

'You sure that's his name?'

Irish stretched and fought down a yawn. 'Pardon me. That is what he told me.'

'That's Mason?'

'Sure it is.'

'*The* Mason?'

Irish shrugged. 'He's a Mason, at any rate. Why? Is he notorious?'

'I thought you said you knew him.'

'I do. I think.'

'He was right about one thing . . . you got to get yourself dressed, mister. I seen all of you I care to see.' She looked back to the fire.

Irish pulled down at the bottom of his soiled nightshirt and got to his feet. 'I was waiting for my clothes to dry.' He felt his face heat up and he had to make water in the worst way. But how far did he dare to go from camp with Mason gone off God knew where. And would the man return? He doubted it. He'd not been the most reliable traveling companion.

He pulled on torn, wrinkled, and dirty pants, shirt, a collar that had lost its stays, one arm garter, an embroidered brocade vest missing most of its buttons, and his scuffed but serviceable low riding boots. He had liked the cut of them with the brown suit in the looking glass at the haberdashery in St. Louis.

He topped off his ensemble with his nearly dry, though oft-crushed, brown bowler. It had been a luxury he knew that all respectable drummers should have. He told himself it would open doors closed to hatless men. The wide brown silk band and ribbed edging had sold him on it. The thing was sorely misshapen and if he had to admit it, had shrunk during the rainstorm. Still, he was relieved to note that the dead girl hadn't taken a liking to it, otherwise he'd be obliged to leave it resting on her face, not like Mason, who wore a hat that had graced the deceased. He shuddered lightly and turned to the girl. 'There now, what do you think?'

'Look like a dandy who's lost his way.'

He straightened and buttoned his shirt cuffs. 'I'll take that as a compliment, thank you.'

'Take it any way you like. I won't tell you how I meant it. But I will tell you that hat ain't right no more. Not that a bowler ever looks right.'

She was obviously still distraught over her sister's death, poor thing. He sat down and poured each of them a cup of coffee. 'You were going to tell me something about Mister Mason.'

She sipped from the hot tin cup, rested her chin on a knee, sipped again, and said, 'If it's him, and I bet it is, he's a legend.'

Irish paused, the cup halfway to his mouth. 'A legend, you say?'

'Yep.'

'How so?'

The girl sipped again and said, 'He's an outlaw. Sort of. The law wants him. But they don't chase him all that hard.'

'Why not?'

She stared at him, wide-eyed. 'You really ain't from these parts, are you?'

'Whatever gave you that impression?'

If she sensed his sarcasm, she didn't let on. 'Nobody knows much about him. Some folks say he's out to get revenge for his family's death. Some folks say he ain't real, more like a ghost or spook or something. I think folks talk to hear themselves talk, say the same things over and over.'

'I can't disagree with you there. My dear old mother — '

'Most everybody does agree that he don't hurt innocent people. He goes after the guilty folks.'

'That's nothing more than vigilantism. And as far as I know, that's illegal, even out here.'

'Mister, ain't nothing illegal out here.'

Irish sipped his coffee and something occurred to him. 'He did tell me that he kills killers. It was funny how that came up, because I asked him — '

'It's him then. It's Mason.' She shook her head and a small smile pulled at her mouth. 'We actually jumped Mason. If Cheery only knew — '

As if on cue, they heard the soft beat of hoofs on the forest floor. They both scrambled to find something to fight with but Mason came into view on Bub.

'Relax, it's only me. Lucky you.' He dismounted and draped Bub's reins over a low branch on which women's wrinkled undergarments waved in a slight breeze. He pretended not to notice them. 'How about some of that coffee.'

He walked to them and said, 'Well, Irish. Looks like you finally decided to cover yourself up. Can't say it's an improvement. Especially that hat. What do you call that?'

Irish handed him a cup and said, 'It's a bowler.'

'I thought so.' Mason sipped the coffee and said, 'Never trust a man in a bowler.' He wrapped his hands around the cup. 'Ahh, nothing like a cup of this stuff to kick the day in the pants.'

His smile disappeared as he watched the two of them pretend the fire was more interesting than anything he had to say. He looked at the girl and said, 'I guess you pretty much told him what you've heard about me.'

The girl looked him in the eye and

said, 'I told him the truth.'

'You told him what you've heard, which is a far shine from the truth, sister.'

'Me and Cheery took to the road because of you. Folks said you always do the right thing and help out the poor folks.'

'Well they got it wrong. People believe what they want to believe, nothing more.'

'But we took to the road because of you.'

'You rob innocent men because of me, too?'

She narrowed her eyes and spoke through clenched teeth. 'You're men, and that sure don't make you innocent.'

'It doesn't make me guilty. Nor him, neither.' Mason gestured at Irish with his cup. Some of it sloshed on the ground. 'He may have godawful taste in clothes and animals, but he's as innocent a tenderfoot as you're liable to find out here.'

She looked back at the fire. 'All we

ever wanted was to be like you.'

'Good, then I'm making the right choice.'

She sat up straight and her scowl deepened. 'I've had enough of you calling me sister . . . mister.'

Mason smiled and waved his arms wide, coffee cup sloshing again. 'Well then, why don't you tell us what we're supposed to call you.'

'She's Belle-Ruth,' said Irish. The girl glared at him. Mason's smile slid from his face. He looked stricken and turned to Bub and his saddlebags, recinching the straps, fiddling with the buckles.

The girl said, 'What's the matter, Mason, cat got your damn tongue?'

He paused, closed his eyes, and in a low voice said, 'I knew a Ruth once. It's a good name. You'd do well to earn it.'

The camp was silent for a time, but for the snorting and stamping of the livestock Mason tended. It was his voice that broke the silence. 'Cayuse Falls is half a day's ride due west. That way.' He pointed a gloved hand at the space in the trees from which he'd ridden.

'I have business there myself. Business that can't wait.' He mounted Bub and said, 'You two'll have to bury the girl and then gather up your things and head on to town.' He rested his hands atop the pommel. 'I'll buy you a hot meal if I see you there.' He touched his hat brim and rode out of camp in the direction he had pointed moments before.

Irish stood there looking after him.

Mason wasn't quite out of sight when the girl turned on him with fight in her eyes, and said, 'How'd you come to know my name?'

'I heard your sister call you that back when you, well, when you robbed me and tied me to the log.'

'Sorry 'bout that.'

'Not to worry. All's forgotten.'

'You remembered my name? After all you've been through? I wouldn't have.'

'It's a pretty name. Nearly as pretty as you.' Irish smiled and looked at her. For the first time since meeting her, she blushed.

He was too busy staring at her reddened cheeks to see the uppercut she landed on the underside of his chin. His jaws snapped together and he looked up at the clearing sky. Then, as that faded, he heard a pretty voice say, 'Another damn man.'

13

He never imagined having such a week. Hell, it wasn't even a full week, just a few bad days. When he'd been within days of reaching the end, he'd nearly been stopped. Waylaid and reduced to stumbling through the woods in nothing but his skin — yes sir, it had been one hell of a few days.

Finally, with the annoying little Irishman and that manhating girl behind him, and with Bub once again under him, his own clothes on him, and even a bit of his own food and coffee in him, Mason continued with the course of action he had set in motion years before.

He glanced at the surrounding countryside, saw the rolling swells of sheepgrass and swale silver in the late morning sun and let Bub lope for a bit. The warmth felt good after being trapped in the gloom of the close, wet forest. He was but half a day's ride east of Cayuse Falls, his horse was sound and his belly was full. Despite the odd nature of his trek, his gut told him this decision was the right one.

He had expected, at the outset of the trip, to come to the end of this thing. He hadn't counted on being slowed down, and he hadn't counted on Pontiff to make a play of this sort. Certainly nothing more than some last-minute whining and offers of bribery. He never expected Pontiff would send an assassin out after him.

Mason realized he shouldn't be surprised. In fact, he should have seen it all along. It was perfectly true to character for Pontiff to hire someone to do his dirty work. He sighed and straightened his back, wincing at the cracking sounds.

As Mason guided Bub down a meandering descent out of the hills and toward the river bottom, he thought of the pretty young blonde girl and her dead sister, who would be alive if not for him. Granted, probably not for much longer, given the life they were leading. He wondered if the young girl or her big sister got off any shots at the killer? Likely, though the girl wasn't in any mood to talk about it. He was pretty sure the killer thought he'd shot Mason and not a big girl wearing his clothes, otherwise he and Irish would have been jumped yesterday.

Mason had tracked him as far from the camp as he was able, but the storm made a right mess of anything that wasn't rock-hard to begin with. If the killer made it back to Cayuse Falls, then what sort of reception could Mason expect from Pontiff? He smiled at the thought. The look on Pontiff's face would almost be worth the long years of waiting. Almost.

Mason reined Bub to a stop and fished his plug tobacco out of his vest pocket. He carved off a ragged hunk and worked the knobby thing to a chewable consistency, all the while thinking of altering his course of action. Not enough to change his final plans but enough maybe to save his skin. Or at least try to prevent an ambush. He nudged Bub into a walk down the slope, but at the bottom he veered south-west, to come into the little river town from an unexpected direction. With a snake like Pontiff, a man couldn't be too careful.

Was a time he would have dealt with a clear-cut wrong in the speediest manner possible. But those days were gone. He had promised himself — and Rita back in Kansas City — all that was a thing of the past. Just as well, too, considering the last few days. He'd been out of the game too long. Hell, he never even liked the game, the tracking of killers, living on the wrong side of the law, being some sort of hero to people with sad lives, trying to make some little thing right out of too much gone wrong. Good riddance to that life, he thought, and smiled, thinking once again of Rita.

He sat straighter in the saddle, spit a tailing, viscous stream dead-center on a fat, round rock and nudged Bub into a gallop. Time's wasting, he thought as they headed for the river valley. One last wrong to right — the one that had started it all, and the only one that ever really mattered anyway.

14

It wasn't until he passed by old Walt Niederlitz, reading this week's copy of the *Cayuse Call* in his usual spot on the polished bench outside Abner T's Mercantile, that Judge Newland Pontiff got his usual beckoning from the old ramrod. Every morning, without fail, Newie would pass the bench, and every morning old Walt would wait until Newie was past, enough so that he'd have to turn around to face him. And then he'd get a light selection of carefully chosen, though surprisingly informative words.

Truth be told, he relied on Walt's interpretations of town doings. He certainly didn't have to head to his office on this side of the street each day. In fact, it was a longer route, but the old man was certainly more reliable and a darn sight more amusing than the rag that drunken sot Timms put out.

On this particular morning, he got a choice earful about one of Skin's boys, Walt wasn't sure which, riding into town early, hell bent and yelling for the doc. Seems he also rousted Hap at the livery for a horse, then took it to his sister's place, and they both high-tailed it to the farm.

Newie considered this. Interesting, to be sure, but hardly useful. Unless it meant that old tightwad Skin had finally come down with the fast and fatal disease Newie'd been wishing on him for months.

The old man snapped the single-sheet paper into an upright position, blocking his face from view, humming to himself and making that damned tooth-sucking noise. Newie knew from experience that Walt wasn't quite through with him, so he waited.

'Seems to me I haven't seen Rip in a day or so. Must be about the town somewhere, though. He is town marshal, after all. Wouldn't be right for our only law to up and vamoose on us.'

Pontiff didn't like this last parting comment today. His morning smile, worn solely for the good folks of his fine town, slid from his face and he made his way down the last step to street level. So what if someone needed a doctor at Skin's place? It was none of his affair, except that if it was Skin, that would surely take the pressure off. But not for long.

What if Skin really was out of the way? He let himself dwell on this practical solution for a few seconds. Long enough to resurrect the smile he'd lost moments before. He stepped, once again fully composed, right in front of that old German woman with the moles all over her face.

'Judge, sir,' Harriet Stimplemeyer said, looking down and blushing. 'Please, I am excuse for all of my rudeness.'

'Nonsense, my dear. It is I who should be more careful.' He tipped his derby and turned his full smile on the woman, particularly as there were several people staring down at them from the boardwalk. Even Walt had lowered his paper.

'Do you know,' said Mrs Stimplemeyer, 'Mr Judge, where is to be found the marshal?'

It was as if a match had been blown out, so fast did his mood leave him. Walt and now this old crow? Too much. It was too much to bear from these people. Didn't they know he was just one man? Didn't they know he was not the marshal's keeper?

'How in the hell should I know?' he growled and stepped square in a mud patch, splashing brown slop all over the woman's clean dress. Her hand went to her face, wiping mud there as well, and several women in the throng of morning shoppers reflexively touched their own faces. Too late to make amends, he decided, and stomped his way up the courthouse steps.

Once inside his office, Newie plunked down in his chair and waited until his breathing calmed down. There was no way he was going to let his emotions get the better of him. Maybe at one time in his life he was like that, but not now. Not with everything that was about to happen.

He cursed himself for letting his mask slip out there in the street. And especially in front of the gawkers. He could not let that happen again. So what if the marshal wasn't back yet? So what if something happened out at Skin's ranch? Didn't mean the two events were related. And besides, the ranch was half a day's ride from where he knew Rip was headed.

Still, it wouldn't matter. If that letter of confirmation didn't arrive soon, and preferably on today's stage like he'd promised it would, then there wouldn't be any public support. There would, however, be public outcry.

He sat up straight in his chair, ignoring the squawk from the springs that usually made him wince. How to head this thing off before he completely lost control of it? He sat, fingers splayed along the edge of his massive desk, nibbling on his bottom lip, and with the surety of movement of a man who has made a final decision, he worked his fountain pen quickly over a fresh sheet of paper.

He paused, the page half-filled, and shook his head. A sound like a growl crawled out of his barely parted lips. He tore the sheet in four pieces and set it aside. Then he slid a fresh sheet from the stack, inhaled, and held his breath as he began filling that page with dense, indigo script, punctuating the effort with smiles and grunts of approval.

Thirty minutes later, after much pausing and scrutiny, Pontiff set his pen down without a sound and stared at his handiwork. He let it air dry, then folded it in thirds, and slipped it into an oblong envelope. From the rear of a top drawer he pulled a dusty green stick of sealing wax. He addressed the envelope to himself and melting an end of the stick, he dripped a coin-size blob on the lip of the envelope and mashed his signet ring twice into it, obscuring the imprint just enough. And then he smiled.

15

'Why, yes, ma'am, I would like another cup of coffee. And a bowl of that deep-dish apple pie I saw. If it's not too much trouble, that is.' The woman nodded, flushed from the heat of the kitchen, and smiled. Her gaze locked his for a second longer than he expected. Then she bustled off.

Mason stretched upright, sighing back to a comfortable position with the full feeling that only comes at the end of a good meal. It had been weeks since he'd eaten that much food all at once and months since he'd eaten food that tasty. Rita was a fine cook, but this woman was a master. He hoped the apple pie was more of the same. He knew that the robust woman who kept glancing at him was the same one who had fed him so well seven years ago. This place had been a tent then, with a board front and packed dirt floor.

He remembered the tongue-lashing she'd given one broken-down old rock hound when he'd tried to toss his spent chaw on the floor. After she had humiliated him she'd kicked him out of the place. Mason didn't remember the exact words but he recalled the place was full of men and every one of them grew red and looked to his own plate, hoping that woman wouldn't turn her glare on them.

He pushed his cup to the edge of the table as she approached with the big black agate coffee pot. He also remembered that she'd taken a full dinner out to the old man she'd evicted from the place. He'd still been there when Mason left, sitting on a tree stump outside and licking the tin plate clean like a dog. Now, she poured his coffee and said, 'Pie'll be ready in a few minutes.'

Two young men clumped in, bumping each other and jostling for a place on stools at the counter. The stout woman serving him lost her smile when she saw the boys and circled around them to get behind the counter.

'What'll it be boys?'

'Coffee,' said one, looking around the room with eyes that didn't track with his head movements. The other nodded and Mason noticed then that they were identical twins, probably mid to late teenage years, certainly full grown, though still like pups in every other way, including how they handled their liquor. They leaned a little too casually on the counter, scanning the room.

'And what brings you two out here, especially on a weekday afternoon?'

'Wasn't nothing else to do back home. Pa says the Lord'll decide now — '

The first elbowed his brother hard in the side and said, 'Don't be tellin' our affairs to the world.'

'But everybody knows Ri — '

The elbow shot out again and the second brother squared off, fists raised, at his twin. Mason guessed they'd been down this road a time or two in the past.

The little barrel of a woman slapped the counter in font of them and they jumped, both looking at her. She leaned close to them and said in a loud whisper, 'There something we should know, boys? Everyone all right out at the ranch?'

The boys stared at each other a few seconds more, Mason saw only the face of the one boy, the one with the fly-away elbows, but he guessed they were both caught between talk and quiet. A decision passed over the nearer boy's face and the shoulders of both relaxed. They shook their heads and the woman stared at them a few seconds more, then said, 'Why don't you boys settle this outside and when you're through, come back in and have some pie. On the house. Hmm?'

The first looked at her, stood full height, and said, 'We don't need no charity.' Then he nodded his head toward the door and they both clumped back out to the boardwalk.

The woman watched them walk out, then a voice from behind her said, 'Pie's ready,' and she disappeared in the kitchen. When she came back out she carried a sizable bowl, steaming on a tray, to Mason.

Steam curled upward through a slit in the pie's crust as she set it in front of him. She rattled a spoon down on the wood table next to it and he closed his eyes and sniffed. Now that was a heavenly smell. 'Ma'am, that is pure perfection in a pie crust.'

'You haven't even tasted it yet,' she said, dabbing her forehead, the tray under one arm.

'If it tastes as good as it smells, I don't know if this old body can stand it.'

She smiled. 'Better let it cool a mite, first. Or you won't be tasting a thing but welted tongue.'

He sipped his coffee. She made to turn away, though he knew, since there were no other customers but two old women in the booth near the front, that she was hoping for a conversation. He'd open the door, see where it led.

'That boy's hard as flint,' he said.

She turned back to him, her eyebrows raised.

'Hard not to hear when it happens right in front of you.' He smiled.

'Oh, that's show. Those boys are all right. They're the Stropworth twins. Now, their father's the one to watch. He's decent enough, but a cheaper man you'll have to look hard to find.'

Mason sipped again and said, 'Sounds like there's something wrong at their nest.'

She nodded and stared at the table top, not really seeing it. 'Something's wrong, I know, because Doc Schmidt and Sue, that's Stropworth's daughter, were called out there early this morning. One of the boys come and fetched them.' Her eyes widened and she said, 'Oh Lord, you watch. It'll be Skin and I'll feel terrible for what I said about the man.'

'Probably kids making more of something than it needs.'

She forced a smile as she headed back to the kitchen. Halfway there she stopped and looked out the big front window.

'Stage is in,' she said to the room. She walked to the kitchen. 'Sure be nice when that railroad finally arrives.'

Mason paused, a first spoonful of pie halfway to his mouth. That Pontiff, he thought, shaking his head. He's got this town wishing for something that'll never happen. What would they do when they found out the truth? What would they do to the man who promised them such things, promised them so much, in fact, that they bet everything they had on the chance?

So help me God, he thought. I know what will happen. He was betting as much on it as these people had wagered on the train running smack dab through their little burg. Only he felt more secure in his own bet. And he never bet unless it was a sure thing. So this time he bet his life on it. He tucked into his pie and tried not to think about Newland Pontiff and the great disappointment that was about to befall nice little Cayuse Falls.

When it came time to pay his bill, he was attended by a young girl no older than those twins. She looked tired already, even though the evening rush had yet to begin. He smiled and thanked her, but he knew how she felt. The pie had been plenty tasty, but Pontiff had wedged himself into his mind and Mason knew there was only one way to get him out. He sighed and headed for the nearest set of batwings to kill a few hours.

16

'Why'd we go in there in the first place, Cal?' Russell batted his brother's arm as they walked up the street.

'I wanted a cup of coffee is all. That stuff Pa makes is so weak it's nearly water. It don't hardly keep my head off the table.'

'Since when did you become such a coffee drinker?'

'I always had a taste for it. Why, I — '

'Shh! You see what I see?'

Calvin shook his head. Russell did have the better vision.

'No, over there, dummy. It's the stage. And look who's crowing like he owns it, too. Come on. We can nab that damn Pontiff before he — '

'Hold on, you know what Pa said. That ain't none of our affair. It's between Pa and Sue and Pontiff, not us.'

'Listen to you, mousin' around. Well, if you ain't got the stomach for it, I do. We're family. Rip's laying back at the ranch, half-dead. You heard what Doc Schmidt said. He might not live through today. Hell, Cal, he might be dead. And that fat little fool is to blame. You were right there when Rip spoke. Pa said it's none of our affair, but when did that ever stop you and me? If what Rip said is true — and you know as well as me that Rip ain't never lied to a man in his life — then this whole blamed town is in for it.'

Russell looked at his twin, a shade of himself, and wondered how they were so alike, but so different in so many ways.

'Yeah, I guess you're right. This town needs a couple of heroes, right?'

'Now you're talking.' He slapped Calvin on the arm and said, 'Let's get him before he waddles back to the courthouse and locks himself away again.'

'Well, what are we gonna say?'

190

Russell grinned and said, 'I have no idea. But when it comes out it's bound to be good. It's me, remember?'

* * *

Pontiff watched as the stage rolled toward Hap's stock yard and livery, which also served as the stage station. Even after all that rain, slight wisps of dust still rose from its departure. There had been no letter, he knew there wouldn't be. He would hire a buggy and drive to Granby himself and wire the railroad office. There had to be a mistake. It certainly wouldn't be the first time a letter had been misplaced or stolen or used as a tobacco spit rag by the shotgun rider.

Yes, sir. If that railroad deal didn't go through, never mind what the town would do to him, he wouldn't give a wooden nickel for this town's prospects. He looked up, wondering whether he should head on over to Margaret's Diner or wait a couple more hours for suppertime. More of a crowd but less chance that Skin would be in — his chores would keep him at the ranch until the next day at best. Unless he had contracted a terrible sickness. Newie smiled and shook his head.

'Newie,' he said in a whisper. 'You are a terrible person sometimes.' He giggled and turned on his heels toward the courthouse, trying not to think of coffee and a steak, mashed potatoes and gravy, thick slabs of homemade bread topped with fresh butter and jam. And he noticed two men walking his way. He half-smiled at them and was raising his hand to wave when it dawned on him who they were. And they were closing in fast.

He had enough time to paste on a smile as wide as his head would allow. Skin must have sent them, he decided, and he reached up to grasp his lapels. He felt the stiff edges of the fake letter inside his coat pocket and his smile grew wider. His eyes glinted sharp and bright, and he even laughed a little as they strode up.

'Boys! Or rather, men! For that is what you've grown to become, fine upstanding young men, able to vote soon, I take it? Ha! Good for you two. I was talking with your father a few days back, business matters, you understand, but he was telling me how very proud he is of you both. And it's a rare day that goes by when I don't have a heart-to-heart with my good and close friend Rip about his extended family. Family by marriage is as near to the real thing as a man will get. He is exceedingly proud of his association with your family, I can assure you.'

He shifted his gaze from scanning the street back to their faces. They towered over him and were glaring at him hard, as if any respect or fear of him had evaporated as he spoke.

'I must be running along, documents for the territorial governor and more for Washington, you know. It's that time of year, my good fellows. Do give your father my best.' Newie started to turn, still smiling, and then spun back, catching the two young men still staring at him, each of them on the verge of saying something. And from the rising color in their cheeks, he guessed it was not something he wanted to hear.

'By the way, boys,' he reached into his coat and slid out the long, buff-colored envelope with the wax seal. 'This came on the stage.' He wagged it in front of his face like an oriental fan. The seal had been broken, the envelope's mouth flopped open. Nice touch, he thought, opening it right at the stage, even if Rupert Almistad, that unwashed buffoon of a driver, was the only one to see. Word would get around.

'It's that blamed letter I've been waiting on. I was going to share it with the town fathers at a special meeting, but if you'd like I'll read it to you. You can pass the news to your father.' He leaned in close to them and said, in a mock whisper, 'Between you and me, it's good news, boys. The best news this town has ever had.' He leaned back and tilted his head to one side. 'And you can thank your Uncle Newie for it, I dare say.'

He lavished indulgence on them with a smile he knew they would carry with them forever, always remembering this adult moment of kindness and confidence in the street.

Like lightning one of the boys batted the letter from his hands and stomped it under the heel of his gnarled old farm boot. 'We don't care about that! What did you do to Rip?'

'Rip?' said Newie, his hands drawn up to his chest, his special smile a thing forgotten. 'What do you mean? He's the marshal, isn't he? That's a good position — '

'That ain't what we mean,' said the other one, closing in on Newie. He looked around but no one had yet noticed this attack. 'Rip's near to dead back at our place. Shot to pieces.'

'What? What are you saying?' Newie's

mind rattled and lurched on its rails. They must be mistaken. They must be drunk. He thought he had detected a whiff of something about them when they approached.

One of the boys leaned in close, the other did the same. 'Rip talked. You want to hear what he said?'

Definitely booze, thought Newie, as he looked up into their angry, pinched faces. He swallowed and nodded.

'Thought you might,' said the first one. He seemed less afraid than the other, though that hardly mattered. He leaned even closer, until the tip of his long, bony nose nearly touched Pontiff's rounded ball of a nose. 'He spoke of you . . . and of Mason.'

Pontiff's legs went to jelly and he thought he was going to drop backward right there in the street. As it was he stumbled backward a step.

The boy nodded, and smiling, said, 'That's right. Mason the Mankiller. Seems he's a friend of yours. Only not anymore. Now he's coming for you.'

Pontiff shook his head. Not possible, not possible. Rip was the best shot around. Rip was a lawman. Rip knew what needed doing. He had everything to gain, same as me. 'That's, that's not possible,' said Newie, his voice quivering like an old man's.

'It's possible, all right. 'Cause Rip said Mason ain't dead. Rip got the wrong one. Only thing we want to know is why a man like yourself, a fine dandy man like yourself,' the boy flicked at Newie's lapel, 'would be in cahoots with a man like Mason the Mankiller?'

Newie tried to swallow but his throat was so dry his tongue rasped in his mouth, filling it with an urge for water. For some reason all his thoughts were of water. He hadn't had such a need for a drink of cool water since he had been on the rock gang in the desert so long ago. All because of Mason . . . And here it was again. Every thought sizzling like bacon on the sun-hot rocks of that cursed desert.

'Hey, you boys, what are you doing

there? What's happening?'

The boys straightened up and looked like scolded kids again, the menacing scowls and lined eyes melting back into the two soft faces of caught children as they looked behind them to old Walt Niederlitz coming out of the alley. He was still fumbling with his suspenders and his old white shirt was half untucked, his paper folded under his arm. 'What in blazes is going on there? Move along, all of you. No sense in you loitering in the street like that.'

The boys looked back to Newie and he saw in their eyes that they wanted to push him, to spit on him, something, anything but walk away and leave him be. But what they didn't know was that leaving him untouched would be worse. At least if they gut-punched him he would have an outward reason to feel so deflated.

They turned away and he grabbed the nearest by the sleeve. 'Mason can't be allowed . . . don't let him get to me. Please . . . ' He knew how this would sound to the young men. He knew and he didn't care. If what they said was true, then he truly was at an end. There was no other recourse.

The railroad, the cattlemen's club, the courthouse, the governorship, and whatever else his future may have held, all for naught. He trembled and felt himself tearing. His eyes focused on the young men staring at him. 'Please, you don't understand. Stop him and I can give you anything you want. I can make your biggest dreams come true. Just don't let him get to me.'

The one whose sleeve he held stared at Newie's pink, pudgy hand and jerked his arm free. They looked at him as if he were smeared with mud instead of wearing his fine Eastern boiled wool suit. Neither of them said a thing as they walked off toward Garvin's Saloon.

'You all right, Judge? Those ruffians didn't manhandle you, did they?'

It took a few moments for Walt's voice to penetrate his daze. Newie looked over at the old man and shook his head. He took a step, then remembered the letter, retrieved it from the dirt, and walked through the sun-cracked mud toward the court-house steps.

17

'You boys think you're up to it?' Scoot Flanders clunked the toe of a cracked work boot against the front of the plank bar and took a step back. He placed both hands, palms down, on the pocked surface. He repeated himself slowly and turned his head, cocked at too much of an angle, and squeezed the gaze from his one good eye at the twins' faces.

'Up to what?' said Russell, standing straighter and trying to look at that eye. He couldn't quite do it.

'That'll do, Scoot.' Sully Garvin, owner and barkeep of the place, frowned at Flanders and shifted the same look to the boys.

As if Garvin hadn't spoken, Scoot said, 'Up to drinking with men, that's what, you damn cur.'

'You know who our father is,

Flanders?' Russell tried a squint of his own.

'Yeah, I know all about you Stropworths.' He waved an arm wide at the sparsely populated room. 'Hell, we all knowed a Stropworth or two in our time.' A couple of the men joined him in ragged laughter.

'I said that's enough. Now go take your chair or hit the bricks, Flanders.' Garvin moved down the bar until he was in front of the one-eyed drunk. The barkeep's impressive height was matched only by his enormous belly, a creature that tested the fabric of his shirt at every seam, and his flowing mustaches, which were greased to drooping points.

He would have done the same to his head hair, but it shone in baldness in the dull afternoon light and the weak flicker of the oil lamp played shadows off his bare pate. He folded his arms, the bar rag still dangling from one big pink fist. Scoot backed from the bar, smiling and offering a slight bow, his head still cocked like a crow's at the twins.

When he was seated, Garvin shifted his gaze to the Stropworth boys once again. 'What might you boys be in here for?'

The twins looked at each other. Russell stretched himself up to his full height, somewhat taller than most of the men in the room. His lack of whisker stubble and fine mustache hair belied his true age. 'I expect we're here for the same reason everyone else is.'

'To have a drink,' said his brother. They both nodded, as if something had been decided. Garvin stared at them for long moments, then a smile twitched his mouth corners. 'Right. What'll it be?'

'Whiskey,' they both said it at the same time. That happened too often, but they didn't seem to be able to help it.

He stared a moment more then plopped two small glasses on the bar in front of them. He reached behind him and pulled the cork from a nearly full bottle of something called Mad Jack's Revenge. He poured the amber liquid to the rim of each glass and corked the bottle. As he turned, Russell grabbed the bottle and said, 'Leave it, friend,' and smiled.

The big bartender worked his jaw muscles and nearly backhanded the young whelp. He'd grown up with their father, hunted with him, come to be wary of him as most others in the town had. For no other reason than he'd become so cheap nothing would please him.

And now his young twin boys come in here, already having tippled something, probably their father's hidden bottle, and were talking to him as though he worked for them. The eyes of the young men were quickly clouding with bravado. Maybe a good hangover was what the scoundrels needed to take the wind from their sails.

He nodded once and set the bottle on the counter between the two glasses.

They were watched as they pinched the vessels between their finger and thumbs as they'd seen men do, peering in over the batwings while their father stopped off for what he called a 'snort' before heading home, once he'd concluded his weekly business in town. He always managed to get into an argument no matter where in town he went and it looked as though they, too, would carry their father's burden with them.

They raised their glasses, not daring to look at each other or in the mirror before them, where they saw the men scattered through the room all staring at their backs and their faces.

They swallowed and for the briefest of moments felt sure they were a cut above other men, so smooth did it go down. There was nothing to this, the grimaces and bullish exhalations they'd seen so often were little more than the paltry displays of soft men. They nearly turned to each other to exchange smiles when the burn ignited in their craws and washed upward like a hot spring.

The raw, searing pain was too much and they sputtered and slumped forward, then down, clutching their windpipes, coughing into their hands.

When the dull noise of their own retching dwindled, it was replaced by a roomful of guffaws and hoots and jeers. The half-dozen patrons, to a man, laughed and pointed at them. Garvin had moved to the far end of the bar and was dunking a dented spittoon in a tin bucket of water on the floor. He looked up at them, shook his head, and went back to his task.

Calvin and Russell stood at the bar, dragging their cuffs across their leaking eyes and noses and trying with no success to look as though nothing had happened. Calvin saw the men in the mirror, the laughter having dwindled, still peeking at them. He looked at his brother and nodded, then filled their glasses again. The noise in the bar stopped.

They each raised their glasses and downed a second shot. And it was better than the first. They plunked down their glasses and the place erupted in cheers. The men at the tables, led by Scoot Flanders, who was standing, smiled and nodded at them in the mirror.

'Come on over, boys,' he said to the twins, catching their eye.

He was met with cold looks. 'I meant men. Come on over . . . men. Join us.' He pushed one chair out with his toe and dragged another from an adjacent table. 'And bring your bottle.'

Within minutes they were the best of friends with the group of fellows at the table. One, whom they recalled from the previous summer's hay gathering, offered to teach them five-card stud.

'What brings you fellers into town on your own? And on a weekday, too.'

Scoot's brazen question paused Russell for a moment and he stared at the man. His brother said, 'Rip's been laid low. We're not sure if he's going to — '

'Shut your blamed fool mouth. What comes upon our family stays in our family. You got that, Cal?'

'What's that about Rip?' said Scoot, leaning close, head cocked like a listening dog, his one good eye wide and skittering between both boys' faces.

'Nothin'. Ain't nobody's business but ours. It's family.'

'If it involves the town marshal, then it dang sure is our business. Why, it's the business of everybody in this town. We're all paying his wage.' He sat back in his chair and spread his hands wide, like he was showing off a fine garment. The men around him nodded.

'Now what is this about Rip, boys?' Garvin had come up behind them. The twins looked up at the massive man, looming over them, then back to their newfound friends, all of whom had edged away and seemed smaller, slighter in their own chairs. Russell found it hard to focus on the question. What had the man asked him?

Garvin grabbed the backs of the boys' chairs and spun them both around to face him. 'What's happened to Rip? Is he hurt?'

And before either one checked with the other, they were both blurting out the story. They soon saw that all eyes were locked on them. They leaned back and expanded on the events, trading turns speaking, nodding in support of one another. Events that, it seemed, each of them had played a major role in shaping, not the least of which was the rescuing of Rip. The twins' sheer brute force and hard riding had saved the man's life and it was up to Doc Schmidt and the good Lord to do the rest.

They filled their glasses and Calvin nodded to his brother, who had a better way with words, they both knew, and Russell proceeded to reveal the kicker: the name of Mason, and how that killer of men fit into the tale. How they had personally heard the horrified utterings of their dear sister's own husband, the very marshal of Cayuse Falls, and how he had been attacked by Mason in broad daylight, then left to die. But the boys, of course, had seen to it that Rip would live to see Mason hang for this heinous crime.

'If I have to spend every last minute of every last day of my time on God's green earth hunting that killer down, so help me, I'll do it,' said Russell. His hat slid off his head and plunked on the floor behind his chair.

The batwings creaked open, slipped shut, and a bull of a man, a stranger, filled the doorway. He looked them over, then strode to the bar and flipped a heavy coin onto the bartop and said to Garvin, 'When you get a minute, barkeep, I'll take a glass of beer.' He leaned against the bar and surveyed the room.

As Garvin walked to the bar, the men turned their attention back to the boys. 'Mason?' said Scoot. 'Can't be. Are you sure? What would someone like that want with little ol' Cayuse Falls?'

18

A small, ancient man in a black suit and mutton-chop sideburns, in a voice like an old hinge, said, 'Heard tell from a man on a train last time I was in Buxton that he knew someone who'd lived through one of those gunfights Mason's always starting. This fella said that you couldn't miss him. Mason, I mean. Thin as a rail, long black hair, and a head taller than any man you're likely to meet. He goes around all duded up in black, head to foot. Even his gun rigs, double and tied down, of course, was all black leather. And jeweled, with silver and gold. Some say from the teeth of his victims. And his horse was black too, like midnight in hell.'

The group was silent. A fat, bearded man in a shabby tan bowler reached for his glass and broke the spell.

'I don't believe it,' said Scoot, helping himself to the twins' whiskey. Neither of them said a thing, too entranced in the spell they'd woven. All eyes were still on them.

'Why don't you believe it?' said the small man. 'I'm not lying.'

'I know you ain't lying, Lemuel, but why would he be here?'

One of the twins smiled then and Scoot said, 'What's so funny?'

The boys exchanged looks, then Russell said, 'We happen to know why he's coming.'

The stranger took a long pull on his beer and wiped the foam from his mustache. He set his hat on the bar and leaned there, his back to the group of men.

'Russell and Calvin, if you know something we should know, then you'd better out with it so we can make sure we protect ourselves. This is no time to play games, son.'

'Since when do you call me 'son'?' Russell faced the bartender with a hard look, then turned back to his friends.

'So?' said Scoot.

'So,' said Calvin. He was tired of his brother getting all the attention. He had been the one to find Rip, after all. 'It's because of . . . Pontiff.'

'What?' said Garvin, coming around the bar again.

'It's true,' said Russell. 'Him and Mason know each other somehow. Near as we figured, Pontiff was trying to get Rip to kill Mason before he got here. But it didn't work out that way.'

Another silence, and then Scoot sat up and slapped the table top. A short stack of poker chips slid and fanned. 'Maybe Rip took care of him, then. They had a fight and Rip shot Mason to pieces before Mason got the chance to kill Rip.'

'Rip?' said a fat, bearded man in a bowler at a nearby table. 'You kidding? He's a nice fellow and all, but ain't no way.'

'He's right,' said Calvin. 'Rip said he missed. Said he shot a woman instead.'

Mason sipped again from his beer and set the glass back down on the worn, polished surface.

'Hey, you, at the bar. Old dad.'

Mason recognized it as the voice of that loud, one-eyed goober who was doing most of the stirring of that little crowd.

'You look like a fella who's been around. Ever seen Mason the Mankiller?'

Mason stayed still, but cut his eyes to the mirror. The men all stared at him. 'If I have, it's been so long I can't rightly say I'd know him anymore.' His voice sounded tired.

He dropped his gaze and sipped his beer.

'Why, for all we know, he's Mason.' It was the voice of the fat bearded man. Mason looked in the mirror and saw all eyes on his back.

'But he isn't,' said the thin, older man. 'I already told you what Mason looks like. There's no missing him.'

'Hey, mister. You Mason?' Scoot

laughed, thinner and tighter than before. The boys all joined in, their laughter a sound that stopped as fast as it began. Mason thought they all looked a little less jolly and a lot more sober than when he'd walked in. The twins were changing from red to white. They'd hit green when that whiskey had a chance to soak into their guts a bit.

Mason watched as they leaned in to the center of the table, gabbling like old ladies at a social. They'd already forgotten him. Within minutes they would splinter and disappear in all directions, each hoping to be the one to first spread the grim news. And then the entire town would know he was coming. They wouldn't know he was already there.

19

By the time Newland Pontiff reached his office door, his breathing was a ragged squeeze and his vision blurred through tears of fear and frustration. He never should have put so much stock in Rip's ability to deal with Mason. Hell, the man was a famous killer. Why should he have expected that Rip, at heart a milktoast of a man, had the ability to gun down such a man?

'Oh Newie, you fool, you fool,' he told himself over and over as his shaking hands rattled the skeleton key in the lock. He saw, too late, that he counted too much on the success of his plans and not enough on plans for dealing with potential failure. For better or worse, at least in the past, that was how he had always operated and it usually served him well. But this time he was well and truly sunk.

He'd let the entire thing drag on for far too long — with the railroad, with the bank, with the building of the court-house and his silly plans for the cattlemen's club, most of all with Mason. So many strings so far out of his reach. And now there was no retrieving them, no tying up a single one.

His office door at last swung wide and he stood there looking in at his desk, his beloved chair, together form-ing the seat of power in which he always envisioned himself. And he'd held that powerful position, too, for several years. But it wasn't enough. And yet it would have to be. And in that moment he knew what he had to do. The perfect solution to his predicament settled on him like bricks from above.

He left the office door open and retreated down the back stairwell to the little storage room by the back alley door.

* ★ ★

He stood on the edge of his desk, as he had for nearly an hour, his knees bent, his shoe-leather creaking as he raised his entire weight up on his toes. His trembling fingers touched again the bulky knot pushing against his right ear. It was not a proper hangman's knot. He didn't know how to tie one. It occurred to him that was one thing, one of many, he would never have the opportunity to learn to do. Not that he'd want to, but while alive the chance to learn something, anything, would always be there. But dead, there were no chances left.

He swallowed and felt the hemp, stiff and itching, against his Adam's apple. His left foot slipped off the decorative sloped edge of the desk and he set his heels down and stood flat-footed on the desktop again. The overhead light fixture swayed, flickering brightness from the three sconces bounced through the room and shadows swung across the floor, corners, and walls, giving the office a grim, cold quality that put him in mind of a funeral parlor.

He trembled all over and his teeth chattered as if he were naked in a blizzard. He wanted to do this. Well, not exactly this, but his options were gone. When they looked at the bank's books, at the loans he'd taken out on behalf of the town and with the town's coffers as collateral, when they realized, as he finally admitted to himself today, that the railroad was not coming to Cayuse Falls, then they, the entire town to a person, would demand his arrest and imprisonment, and that would be the end for him.

He could not, would not, go back to that hellish prison where he had spent what felt like a lifetime. He was tired of fighting for every scrap, tired of living as if every second some unwanted thing from his past was set to lunge at him. It was no way to live. And prison was no way to live. And since those were the only options open to him in this mortal world, then the last option was his for the taking.

Maybe that talkative dove in Alamera had been right. He'd thought off and on through the years about what she'd said. He didn't remember much of anything about her. Nothing that struck him as special, except what she had told him as he was getting dressed. Maybe we do come back to this world as something else alive and new. If so, he hoped it wouldn't be as a little fat man named Newie Pontiff. Not again. And definitely not a farm animal. Or anything rented out of a livery. Maybe a wolf or a hawk. They looked as though they had pretty good lives. He fixed his mind on a set of wings in a clear blue sky.

'In for a penny,' he whispered. His leg muscles tightened and he gritted his teeth.

The big door's glass knob rattled and he heard a muffled voice growl. Pontiff opened his eyes and the door pitched inward, its stiff weight slamming into the bookcase behind. And there was Mason, the swaying light from the fixture raking his massive form, his gun drawn. He was larger than he'd ever been in Pontiff's mind.

'Oh, no, you don't,' growled Mason, his pistol aimed at Pontiff's chest.

For what seemed an hour the two men, bitter enemies for years, and this their first meeting since the incident so long ago, faced each other, the light swinging in wide arcs about the room as Newie's occasional spasms transferred to the rope and then to the fixture. The light wavered, flashing first on one face, then the other. Newie, his eyes narrowed and sharp, his hands on his chest as if he were about to sweep crumbs from his shirtfront, and Mason, his face red, his eyes and nostrils wide, a smile not quite showing itself.

It was Pontiff who broke the silent stand-off. 'Why would you want to stop me from doing what you yourself want to do?' asked Pontiff in a light, questioning tone.

Mason didn't answer. And then he smiled. 'You answered your own question.'

Pontiff wobbled on the desktop, the light wagged. He said, 'Oh, hell,' and with a hop he pushed off the desktop. For less than a second he arced forward toward the far corner of the office. Then, at the end of his swing, he felt the rope tighten about his neck and he heard a tremendous ripping and crunching, felt a streak of heat blaze from his groin on up to the back of his head, then blackness, and he knew no more.

* * *

Mason thumbed a match alight and touched it to the wick on an oil lamp. He replaced the globe and twisted the lever until half the room glowed with a warm light. He lifted the lamp from the sideboard and approached the prone man on the floor, where he squatted and held the lamp close to the man's face. Pontiff was out cold, the steel light fixture, inches from his head, had torn loose from the ceiling beam when it felt the fat man's full weight. The one lamp that had remained lit when the fixture came down, had crashed such that the flame lay away from its source of fuel, guttering its last near the carpet.

Mason stood and said, 'Hey.' He toed the fat man's shoulder, repeating the word and the soft kick until the man roused.

Pontiff coughed and gagged, the rope stuck halfway up his head, compressing his cheeks and ears into a pursed look that made him look even fatter than he was.

He struggled to sit upright and clawed at the rope. Then he saw Mason. 'What happened?' he asked, as if they were chatting over coffee. His voice was rough edged.

'You're too fat to hang, Newie Pontiff.'

As if he'd been slapped, Pontiff looked all about him at the mess and then grunted to his feet. He stood facing Mason, and smoothed his suit, tucked in his shirt tails, and keeping his eyes on the big man, wobbled back behind the desk. Mason still held the pistol on him.

Pontiff pulled a bottle off the sideboard and fumbled for a glass. The neck of the bottle clinked the little glass as he poured. He set down the bottle, picked up the drink, and said, 'You want a drink?'

Mason shook his head once. Pontiff shrugged and poured himself another. This seemed to restore some of his bluster. The men stared at each other.

'You're going to blame me for making you what you are, right?' said Pontiff, coughing. 'You're going to say I am the cause of you becoming a cold-blooded killer.' Pontiff slapped the words down between them as if they were a winning hand.

'It's interesting you say that. Interesting you think that. Which tells me something about you. And it's true that if you hadn't ruined my life years back, odds are I would have led a considerably different life. Would probably have my own spread paid for by now. Odds are that would have happened. Or something equally as bad to me and mine. Disease, maybe. Accident.'

He looked into Pontiff's eyes and said, 'A real accident. But no, Newie, I don't blame you. I take full responsibility for what I am, for better or worse. The same thing deep inside me that wants to put down mange-ridden curs who only take from society and never give anything good back, the same thing in me that barely feels regret when I pull the trigger or plunge the blade or tighten the noose or squeeze the neck with my bare hands is the same thing that my Ruth fell in love with so many years ago. So the way I am was chiseled in stone long before I ever met you . . . Pontiff. Don't give yourself so much credit.'

'What are you going to do with me?' said Pontiff. 'It's already known by some of the fools in this town that you're on your way here. I can't fully protect you, but I can offer a chance that you can ride on out in the cover of darkness. I'll keep the posse at bay as long as I can.' He stretched himself full height and said, 'I still have considerable pull here, you know.'

'That why you're looking to stretch your own neck, Newie?'

Pontiff touched trembling fingertips to the glass rim, then grasped it in both hands and raised it, spilling and jiggling, to his lips like a parched man.

'That's what I thought,' said Mason. 'Besides,' he gestured toward the window. 'Your 'people' have already figured out that you and me go way back, Pontiff. And from what I heard, they don't like that idea much. They're beginning to put two and two together. And when they do . . . well, I wouldn't want to be you.'

Pontiff's face lost all color and he said, 'You . . . you told them?'

Mason tilted his head to one side and said, 'For someone who's supposed to be so gifted, you surprise me, Newie. If I had told them, would I be here? Even

Mason the Mankiller wouldn't stand a chance against a mob of angry citizens. How about you, Newie?'

'What do you want from me, then? If it isn't to kill me, what is it you want?'

'Why, Newie, I thought you'd know by now.' Mason stared at the little fat man, his eyes smiling, standing at his ease.

Newie shook his head slowly, like a child.

'I just stopped by to watch you squirm. I don't believe you've done quite enough of that yet.'

20

'Two of the orneriest, most God-awful loud creatures in existence,' said the man, staring at the sullen figures of Nubbin and Florence. Then he directed the same gaze at Irish. The little man knew events of the past few days had taken a toll on his fine clothes, but really, this fellow's bald look of disgust was hardly justified. After all, the stableman's own clothes were stained specimens, ripped and ragged.

'I'll take my business elsewhere,' said Irish, surprising himself with his stern, decisive tone. He'd taken all he would take from others this day. As much as he would have liked to get to know her, Belle-Ruth was prickly and prone to fisticuffs, an undesirable trait in a girl. Knocking him unconscious and leaving him alone in the wilderness was the final straw.

'Didn't mean I don't want your custom. I usually have to get a little extra. For two such animals, you see. 'Sides, there ain't no other place to take them.'

Irish nodded and handed over another half-dollar. 'I'll be back later to check on them. No offense, but they're used to me bidding them a good night.'

The stableman looked at him as though he were a sawdust doll come to life.

'Now,' said Irish, ignoring the gormless man's stare, 'The girl who just left.'

'What girl?' said the stableman.

'Come now,' said Irish, sighing and clinking his coin purse. 'I can see one of her horses in the barn behind you. The other, I presume, is still carrying the body?'

The dirty man swallowed and said, 'Uh huh.' But didn't take his eyes from the slow shake of the money bag.

'Where's the funeral parlor?'

The man pointed back up the road to a dimly lighted storefront. Irish just made out a big horse tied out front, probably the one that carried Cheery.

Irish nodded. 'Do you recommend a place for a bit of a bite and a nice drink?'

'The diner for your food needs. She's packed to the walls this time of night, but Margaret'll find a place for you.'

'How about a quieter place?'

'Falls Hotel's the place for dandies. Got a bar, too. But everybody goes to Garvin's for drinkin'.'

'Thank you kindly.'

So, thought Irish as he strolled from the livery, *the man thinks I'm a dandy*. He smiled. Well, there were worse things to be called, he knew that only too well. He couldn't see much of himself in a mercantile window, but he did linger to admire the goods displayed there. Much, he knew, might be discovered about the health of a town's economy by the goods moved in and out of a shop's front door.

So far, he liked what he saw of Cayuse Falls. He had expected a run-down little town like others he'd been through, though he'd only been peddling his wares less than two months. If he could convince the Professor to stake him for a replacement batch of nostrums, tonics, and tinctures, perhaps he might set up shop right here on this fine little main street.

Up ahead, light and the noise of voices spilled from the swinging doors of a saloon. Since he had a general and lifelong aversion to fisticuffs, he usually avoided common saloons, but it was barely dark and the voices didn't sound angry.

He'd decided to venture in for a drop of the *uisce beatha*, the water of life, when two tall men clunked out, weaving slightly and talking together. He had no interest in being molested. He was too tired, he knew he looked terrible, and he felt worse than he looked. He'd let them go by and then he'd be on his way. They clunked toward him on the wooden boardwalk, then before they reached him they plunked down, side by side, on a bench not six feet from where he stood in the deepening angle of the alley's shadow.

'Why'd you make me leave? I was having some fun — '

'Shut up. Listen, did you hear what that girl said to Garvin? We got it all wrong. Mason's already been killed.'

Irish's gut tightened. He bit the inside of his bottom lip and forced himself to keep quiet. It couldn't be true. Couldn't.

'How do you know that?'

'One of Margaret's kitchen girls, I think it was that Tilly girl from out on the Creek, she brought supper to Garvin — '

'I hate him,' said the other.

'Shut your mouth and let me finish. So the Tilly girl brings Garvin's supper. I heard her telling him she heard from Hap, 'cause she brought him supper from the diner, too, that some girl brought Mason's body in. Hap seen it with his own eyes. Says he's a big'un.

All draped across the saddle like a dressed bear.'

'How's he know it's him?'

'Ain't no one else it could be. No one else was expected here, was they?'

'So . . . don't mean it's him.'

'But Rip let on as how he'd shot a woman by mistake, right?'

'Right.'

'So, a woman brought the body in.'

'So,' said the other one.

'So that can only mean that Rip didn't hit the woman as he thought but shot the man who she was traveling with.'

'Don't mean it's Mason.'

'It does if she says it's him.'

'Did she say that?'

'Well, no. But if she did, would that convince you?'

'Yeh, I reckon it would at that.'

'Well, what are we waiting for? Let's us go find that girl.'

'Keep your boots on. I didn't get to finish my drink.'

Irish felt relief flood through him. Mason was not dead, according to this news. But they also knew of Belle-Ruth. It was only a matter of time before these two drunks caught up with her. And then what?

'Forget the drink. I didn't tell you, but Hap said she's a pretty little thing.'

'Yeah, but if she's Mason's woman, that means she might be as bloodthirsty as him. What sort of woman would travel with a known killer, anyway?'

'You saying she might be a shooter, too?'

'All I'm saying is it might pay to be careful, is all. Two of us should be able to take the starch out of her, if you know what I mean. And then we can drag her off to the jail house.'

The first speaker perked up and said, 'Hey, that's right. Rip ain't here anyway. Somebody's gotta take care of the law end of things in Cayuse.'

The second snorted and said, 'Sure as heck ain't Pontiff. Not if he's in cahoots with Mason. Or was. So it might as well be the Stropworth boys, right?'

They stood and leaned against each

other, then clumped off the sidewalk in the general direction of the livery.

Their laughter faded into the night. Irish, unnoticed in the shadows, let out a long breath. If they had been sober they most certainly would have seen him. What to do? For a moment he considered finding Mason. He seemed a decent sort. He wouldn't let anything happen to Belle-Ruth. Would he?

Those men were heading after Belle-Ruth under false information. It wouldn't take them long to find her, even if they were a bit tipsy. And no one but he and Belle and Mason knew the truth. But Mason was nowhere to be seen. He had intended to find Mason either tonight or early in the morning. He had liked the man but felt that there was something left unsaid by their parting. Mason was troubled, but Irish didn't believe half of what Belle had told him about the man — it was plain that her story was more myth than fact. And while those men confirmed that there was a fair bit of mythologizing to his story, there was also fear there.

And what was more, if they thought that Cheery Girl's body was Mason's, they either didn't know what he looked like and so didn't know if he was in town and among them, or they did know but they hadn't yet seen him. So how was he supposed to find him? And more importantly, how could he protect Belle-Ruth? Those two men would surely find her before long. So he had to locate Belle-Ruth first. It would be the funeral parlor, then the hotel.

As he scuttled down the wood sidewalk, he almost tripped over the outstretched legs of an old man slumped and resting in a chair at the end of the boardwalk.

'Ho, ho, there. Where you headed in such a hurry, fella?'

'I'm . . . I'm looking to find my cousin. I was told he was here. Perhaps you know of him? Pontiff is his name.' Irish hoped that was enough information. He didn't know the man's first name.

The old man reeled his long legs in and sat upright, his newspaper in his lap. 'Well now, why's everybody want the judge all of a sudden?'

'Why, who else has been after him?' asked Irish. 'Was it a big fella?'

'It was. And right polite, too. He said — '

'Where can I find Pontiff?'

'Keep your hair on, fella. I'm getting to that. Say, you're an Irishman, ain't ya?' The old man didn't look like he was too impressed with Irish, but he pointed to a lighted window on the second floor of a new, tall wooden building, clock tower and all, at the head of the street. 'That's him up there. Hard worker, is that one. We're lucky to have him.'

'Thanks for the help. I must dash.' Irish turned and ran in the opposite direction, away from the old man and the gleaming new building.

'Hey, where you going? I told you he's up there,' said the old man, still pointing at the lit windows of the courthouse.

But Irish was headed back toward the hotel he'd passed on his way to the saloon, the hotel the stableman had said he'd directed the girl to. It was closer than the undertaker's, so he'd try there first. He hoped dawdling as he did with the old man didn't mean he'd put Belle-Ruth in jeopardy with those two men. And why did the old man seem so impressed with this Pontiff fellow when it seemed everyone else wanted to see him dead?

21

As his left foot touched the hotel's front step, Irish winced and pulled his head down when a pistol shot cracked the stillness of the dusky hour. His first thought was that he should get out of this town while he still could. It was fast becoming a town he had expected. His second thought was of Belle-Ruth and the men who had left the saloon before him. Keeping low, Irish minced up the side of the staircase and advanced on the still-closed lobby doors.

The frosted glass panes showed little more than shadows moving behind them. He dropped to his knees and wedging himself between a small drinks table and a rocking chair, he peered through a side window. Belle was in there all right. He heard her voice, muffled, barking sharp words. Her back faced him and through the gauzy, lace curtains he saw her gun hand wagging a pistol, pointing like a finger with an emphasis that accompanied her muted words.

Beyond her he made out a man in white shirtsleeves and garters. And he sported slicked hair and an oiled mustache. Probably the desk clerk. Good. It seemed like she was the one who had shot. He looked behind him, but no one had been attracted by the sound of the shot.

He knee-walked to the doors and staying well to one side, reached for the knob. It turned in his hand. He was yanked forward and fell halfway across the threshold. He stared at boots that seemed familiar, and a voice said, 'What in hell are you playing at?'

He looked up and was lost in the furrowed brow and scowling face of Belle-Ruth. Lank strings of blond hair hung about her face and her hat was pulled down low.

'Now Miss Belle-Ruth, I have to talk with you. It's rather urgent.' Irish rose to his feet and noticed the angry-looking man he'd seen through the curtain. He was dapper, though his oiled hair and shoulders were covered with debris and powder, like crumbly gravel had been flung all over the counter behind which he stood, his hands atop it as if he were awaiting a meal. 'Oh, hello, sir,' said Irish.

The man nodded. 'You know her?' he said, nodding his head once at Belle-Ruth.

'Ah, well, yes. Yes, I do.'

'Then kindly tell her not to shoot any more holes in my ceiling. It's a good thing the town's not busy or I'd probably have a dead guest in the room upstairs.'

'There wasn't nobody up there,' said Belle-Ruth.

'That's not the point,' said the man, his nostrils flexing and a sneer pulling his mouth downward.

'We need to talk,' said Irish to her in a low voice. 'There are men coming who wish to do you harm. They're under the impression that your sister is Mason. Or rather that she's Mason's body. You understand me, I'm sure.'

'What are you talking about? I'm trying to get information out of this fool and he won't tell me nothin'.'

'Because there's nothing to tell!' The man looked ready to scream.

'Now, now,' said Irish, putting his arms up, palms facing each of them. 'I don't have time to coddle you both. You'll have to listen to me.' His voice was louder than he expected. 'Belle, we don't really have the time for you to haggle with this man about the price of a room — '

'That's not what I was asking him.' She jerked the pistol at the hotelier. He didn't flinch.

Irish ducked and said, 'There's no time for this, Belle-Ruth.'

She set a locked jaw at him. There was not doubt, only determination, in her eyes.

'There are two men — and soon to be more — coming to find you. They think you're Mason's woman, as they said. And they're convinced you're as bad as he is believed to be. They don't know about your sister.'

'Well, let them come, then!'

Irish said, 'I've seen you shoot, Belle-Ruth.' He looked up at the ceiling. She and the hotelier did the same. 'I'll guess you weren't aiming for the plaster, were you?'

She shook her head and sighed. 'Let's go.'

'Is there a back way out of this place?' said Irish.

'What about my ceiling?'

'What about it?' shouted Belle-Ruth, waving the pistol at him.

'We'll be back to square up with you,' said Irish.

'Like hell we will. He didn't tell me who was responsible for shooting Cheery.'

Irish grabbed her elbow and headed out of the well-lit front room and toward what he hoped was the back of the building. He had in mind a back-alley door, most likely off a kitchen.

'I know who is responsible for shooting her. And I can tell you it wasn't the hotelier.'

She tensed, said, 'Who — ?' and tried to stop, but he kept pushing her ahead of him toward the back of the building.

To his surprise she trotted in front of him. The passage was an unlit hallway and the door at the far end was nearly closed. 'Keep trotting, girl, or we're both sunk.'

And, as if on cue, from behind he heard man-shouts — one, two voices, possibly more, joined by another — the hotelier? Then heavy boots behind them. 'Hurry up, girl,' barked Irish, and he pushed her through the doorway. He slammed the door and groped for a latch, anything that might slow them down. There was a deadbolt under the knob. He slid it into place and said, 'Go, go to the alley,' for they saw oblique light from other lamps, other windows, reflecting through those in this room.

The voices grew louder and fists collided with the door behind them. The knob worked back and forth, rattling. 'Go around!' said a voice, followed by receding boot clunks.

Irish didn't wait for the inevitable sound of a boot splintering the white door. He shoved through the outer door after Belle and said, 'We have to keep moving. They've sent someone around to trap us.'

The blonde drew her pistol again and said, 'I ain't running.'

Before even he knew what he was up to, Irish grabbed the pistol from her hand and said, 'But I am.'

'You can't use one of them,' said Belle, as they stumbled across the alley and into the heavy shadow of a back shed.

'I never said I couldn't. I only prefer not to.'

'Well, ain't you just about some-thing.'

'I am at that.' Their whispered exchange drew to a close as a man, less than twenty feet away, rounded the corner of the large building. He was mostly shadowed, but Irish saw for a moment the outline of a drawn pistol.

The man stepped slowly, crunching in drying dirt toward the short steps they just vacated. Irish guessed it was one of the two men from the saloon. He heard the whisper of Belle's breath at his ear. Despite their predicament he felt his face heat up. Grit ground between the man's bootsoles and the drying hard-pack of the alley. He kept low as he walked.

From inside came the continued pounding of fist against door. The hotelier must be in there, preventing them from breaking down the door. The man reached the steps. Belle-Ruth pushed past Irish, and stepped out of the shadow.

'Psssst!' she hissed.

The man spun and Irish saw the gun fully. It was aimed at Belle. He acted before he thought and got an arm around Belle's midsection to pull her backward as he leveled the pistol at the man.

'Don't shoot!' yelled Irish, but the man's gun barked flame. Something whistled close and Belle yelped and dropped to the ground. Irish fired barely a second after the man. The man yipped like a coyote and dropped where he'd stood.

The pungent, stinging odor of gunsmoke hung in the air. Even though his ears were ringing, Irish heard the intensified thudding and yelling from behind the room's inner door. Belle was on her knees, and he bent to help her stand. His hand touched her arm. It was wet, sticky. 'You've been shot.'

'To heck with it. Let's go!'

He helped her to her feet and they ran up the alley in the opposite direction from where the man had entered. Behind them Irish heard the white door give way. Boots on wood, then shouts. They would be following before long, he knew.

'Why did you do that?' said Irish.

'Do what?' she grunted as he guided them between two close-set buildings.

'Why did you attract his attention like that? We were hidden and he was going inside.'

'Exactly. Pretty soon he would have had his friends out here with us. Then we'd have to shoot 'em all. Why'd you push me out of the way? I had him dead to rights!' Even in the dark, Irish felt the intense glare of those pretty blue eyes boring into him.

'I didn't know you had a gun,' he said.

'You think I'd let you have my only gun? I'm wearing Cheery's two-gun rig.'

He struggled to gain control of his breathing, afraid their location might be given away by their combined sounds. Belle held her arm tucked in front of her.

'How bad is it?' he asked.

'I think it grazed me.' She inhaled sharply. 'Hurts like hell, though.'

'I'm sorry about this, but there was

no time. Still, I should have handled it differently.'

'Oh, hush, and let's get us out of here.' She brushed past him and headed toward the far end of the gap.

'My boy! What have they done to my boy?' The voice, a ragged bellow, reached them from far behind. Belle said nothing, though Irish was sure she heard it, too.

★　★　★

A few minutes later the panting hotelier launched himself through Garvin's saloon doors. They wagged like living things behind him.

'There's a woman and some little foreign fella come running through my place, bustin' up everything in sight. Them Stropworth twins took off after 'em, but I think one of 'em got shot in the alley. Skin's with 'em. He come into town lookin' for them.'

It was as if he'd thrown dynamite into the room. Men and tables and chairs all moving at once.

'What do you mean? Those boys were just in here.' Garvin bellowed across the bartop, but he, too, moved toward the door, ushering the stragglers out into the night.

22

Scarcely two minutes after their scuffle, Irish led Belle-Ruth to the alley behind the courthouse. It was the only place he thought he might find help — if he found Mason. They made it into the shadows close to the big, fresh-wood smelling building and paused there, breathing hard and staring down the street, where lampglow was increasing.

'I have to get you to a doctor and then I'm going to help Mason,' he whispered to her. 'It's a matter of time before they figure out who he is. They already know this Pontiff fellow is in the game with him — '

'Wait, did you say Pontiff?' Belle-Ruth said through gritted teeth.

'Yes,' said Irish. 'That's what the man told me. Odd name, that, but there it is.'

'That hotel fella said that very name

to me. I didn't know what he was on about, but that was the name he used.'

'In reference to what?'

'What kind of talk is that?' Belle-Ruth said, examining her arm. 'You educated or something?'

'Something,' said Irish. He was relieved to hear she'd not yet lost that biting sense of humor.

'I asked who would want to see Mason dead and he said it was rumored that Pontiff was in cahoots with Mason once upon a time, but now he wants him killed. Which fits, because Mason's a outlaw.'

'Be that as it may, you've no business continuing until you've seen a doctor. That arm is bleeding.'

'And you got no business telling me — '

That was all he heard. Irish turned from staring toward the front of the hotel to see Belle-Ruth slumped unconscious on the ground by his feet. He slapped her cheeks and repeated her name with no response. He hoped it was only unconscious. She'd been grazed in the arm. What if it was worse than that?

He straightened her legs, leaned low over her face, and whispered, 'Belle-Ruth, can you hear me?' He paused, listened. She still breathed, light and warm on his face. He squeezed his eyes tight and then looked straight up and whispered, 'Lord, forgive me for what I'm about to do.' And he peeled back the flaps of her coat, peering close to see if she'd been shot elsewhere.

He touched her gingerly about the torso. No wounds that he saw or felt. Distant shouts caused him to pause, his hands on her belly. She moved her head, groaned. He whipped his hands back as if he'd rested them on a cherry-red stove lid.

Irish dragged her as best he could into the shadows by the back door. Then he whispered, 'Good luck to you, pretty lady. Wish me luck, too.' And he mounted the back steps, knowing that the glowing office lights he'd seen earlier, pointed out by the old man, were somewhere up above him. He prayed he wouldn't be too late to help Belle and to warn Mason.

A stairwell rose out of the darkness to his immediate left as he entered the unlocked door. And so he held the pistol out in front of him, and took the steps one at a time, not too slow, not fast enough to clunk his boots and cause alarm. Was he making a mistake by leaving her in the alley, untended, unconscious, and bleeding? Probably. But was he doing it for a good enough reason? He hoped so.

At the top of the landing, he saw a closed door, again to his left. He was quiet, crouching and listening. No sound from beyond the closed door. Was it the right office? It had to be. It was on the correct side of the building, it was the correct floor. He stood slowly and peered closer. At eye level a sign on the door read, 'Hon. N. Pontiff.' *Can't get much closer than this*, he told himself. *Except from inside the office.*

The question is, in like a lion or a lamb?

He inhaled, let out a silent breath, and felt for the knob. As he turned it and pushed inward with all his strength, he also let out a yell and kept low, pushing his weight against the swinging door. Halfway into the dimly lit room, the door met resistance and at the same time his right boot toe caught on the threshold. His chin slammed the floor, bouncing his head hard enough to set off a ringing in his ears. He tried to rise.

Behind him grew an angry, loud sound like a bull, footsteps, more loud grunting, then he felt a heavy hand on his back that pushed him back down flat to the floor, squeezing the air out of him as if he were a bellows. Heavier steps bolted out the door.

It took a few seconds for Irish to focus his vision. He slowly rose to a kneeling position. The room lost most of its motion. Cheery's pistol was still on the floor where his arm had slapped down. Whoever was in the room had left in a hurry. Then his thoughts returned to Belle-Ruth. What if she was found? Whoever was in here was sure to vacate the building.

He had no time for further thought on the matter. Heavy steps sounded on the stairs, ascending, drawing closer. He snatched up the pistol and struggled to his feet, gripping the edge of the big desk.

'Hold it.'

Irish froze in mid-lunge, trying at least to get around the side of the desk. No such luck. But that voice . . .

'Drop the hogleg, and turn around.'

It was.

'Mr Mason,' said Irish as he turned to face the big man in the doorway.

'Irish,' the big man said, advancing. 'I might have known.'

Irish smiled and something huge lashed out in the dark, snapping him across the jaw. His head buzzed and rang again and he doubled over. 'What are you doing, man?' he said through a swelling cheek.

'I could ask you the same thing, greenhorn.'

'I came to warn you. The town's full of men who want to see you dead. They know you're here. Or soon will.'

'You caused Pontiff to escape.'

'Didn't you hear me, Mason? They're after you. Probably going to string you up. I shot a man because of you. And Belle-Ruth's been shot, too.'

Mason grabbed Irish by the arms. 'What? Well, why didn't you say so, Irish? Where is she?'

Irish shook himself free of Mason's grasp and rubbed his jaw again. 'She'll be all right, I think. Grazed her arm, it did. She's unconscious outside. In the alley. I had to leave her there to come get you.'

Mason eased back on the hammer of his pistol and holstered it. 'What do you mean you shot someone?'

'She caused a stir at the hotel. We were chased, and now we're wanted, same as you.'

'Hardly, Irish. Hardly.' The big man was silent a moment, rasping a hand across his jaw. He looked up at Irish as if he just realized he was there. He crossed to the sideboard and rattled the top from the crystal decanter and splashed a healthy dose into each of two glasses.

'Here,' he said, handing one to Irish. 'It'll help that jaw.'

They each swallowed long. Distant sounds brought their glasses down at the same time.

'They've come,' said Irish. The sounds were louder. They were the shouts of men, the words still unclear, indistinct, and muted, blurring with each other, but they weren't the sounds of laughter. 'I told you, Mason. They've come for you.'

'They've come for somebody, but I doubt it's me. More likely it's Pontiff. Word's getting out that he's associating with the criminal element.'

'But men from the saloon mentioned you.'

'They did, did they?' Mason smiled, knocked back the last of his slug, and said, 'But they don't know who I am. Not many do. Except you and the little sister, out there.'

'Belle-Ruth! If they find her . . . I have to go.'

Mason nodded. 'Go help her. Get her out of here.'

'But what about you?'

'What about me?'

'Will you be all right? I could stay and help you — ' Irish shrugged and hefted the big pistol.

Mason's smile wasn't quite hidden in the low lamp light of the room. 'I appreciate that, Irish. But I came to Cayuse Falls because something needed doing. And I'm not leaving until it gets done.'

'But — '

'Get that girl and get out of here.' He grabbed Irish by the shoulder and pushed him out the door and toward the stairs.

Irish paused at the top of the stairs

and said, 'I'm . . . sorry about Pontiff.'

'Oh,' Mason waved a hand. 'That rat'll turn up. The crowd will see to it that he doesn't get far. Now go tend that girl, for Pete's sake.'

23

Aware that Pontiff, a man he'd never seen, was probably still in the building, Irish weighed speed with caution as he felt his way down the courthouse's back stairway. The whiskey sat like a steaming coal in his gut, radiating heat outward and filling him with a renewed vigor. Especially after the rapping he'd given his chin on the floor, and then the backhanding Mason had delivered to his face. His cheek still stung.

He reached the alley door without incident, and crouching, pushed open the door. The waver of many voices came to him, though they didn't sound all that close. He bent low and pushed the door wider with his head. The voices came from the front of the building. He drew in a full breath and scampered through the door. Even before he reached the spot where he left Belle, he knew she was gone. He crouched there, the faint whiff of a nearby outhouse twitching his nostrils.

'Belle?' he whispered. No response. 'Belle-Ruth?' Still nothing. He shook his head at his own folly.

At the mouth of the alley lantern light flickered with eye-blink speed off the raw clapboards. He made his way to the front corner of the building and peeked around it. There were perhaps eight men, most of them looking like they'd come from the saloon. Not as many as he expected. Of Belle he saw no sign.

A clicking like bones breaking sounded just behind him. Irish froze. A voice as cold and hard as a gravestone said, 'Don't you turn, Pontiff. Hands up and drop the pistol.' It was a woman's voice.

That the voice was directed at him he had no doubt. But if he didn't say something soon he would end up dead. He might not know what this Pontiff looked like, but he was not a well-liked man.

'Belle?'

'Who?'

'You'll pardon me, but I'm not — '

'That's enough talk, Pontiff.'

'But I'm not — '

The hammer locked back one last click, settling into its deadly role. Whoever she was, he hoped she would not shoot a man in the back. But the venom in her voice showed a real hatred for Pontiff. Something beyond anger that made the voice quaver in rage. Given everything that had happened over the past few days because of Pontiff, Irish thought he would like to pummel him, too. And so, he supposed he was no different than anyone else in Cayuse Falls.

He heard shoes on gravel and then something hard like a steel finger, the barrel of a gun, rammed into his back. He didn't dare utter another word.

'Walk. Toward the street.' There it was again, that tense edge, like a train close to skipping track. He prayed to his mother that this woman wouldn't trip and shoot him. She sounded tired. Angry, to be sure, but tired as well. He walked toward the flickering lantern light and the voices of the clustered men.

They were within twenty feet of the men when they were noticed. 'Who's that?' said one of them, turning to face them, a hand gripping a holstered pistol, the other held out, testing the air as one might test water before wading deeper. 'That you, Pontiff?'

The men squinted into the dark toward Irish.

'Please don't shoot,' said Irish. 'Give me a chance to explain.' It was then that the woman behind him, who still hadn't been seen, spoke up.

'Clear out of the way, you men. I aim to kill Pontiff right in front of his damn courthouse.'

'Sue?' said one of the squinting men. 'That you, Sue McCorkle?'

The pressure from the gun in his

back eased and the woman behind him stopped walking. 'Who said that?' she said.

'It *is* Sue. Sue, your brother Calvin has been shot out back of the hotel. Your father's with him. So's Doc Schmidt.'

'No, I ain't neither,' came a booming voice from behind the men, moving closer. It was Skin Stropworth striding forward out of the dark with determined steps, a gunbelt on his waist and a rifle in his hand. In thc distance, lanterns and oil lamps were held aloft, casting wavering orbs of light on clothes and peering faces. 'Cal's gonna make it,' he said to those near him. 'Russ and Doc Schmidt are with him.'

One of the men said, 'Skin, that's Sue over yonder. She's got a gun on that fella there. She thinks he's Pontiff.'

'It *is* Pontiff,' she shouted. Irish heard the rage shaking her voice, cracking its limits.

'Sue, what are you doing here?' said Skin in a strained voice. 'Rip needs your care. I left you with him so I could fetch home the boys.'

'Rip's dead.' She said it loud and with clipped finality. Silence, like that after a harsh face slap, stilled the street.

'What?' wheezed Skin. 'No, no. It can't be. We seen him a few hours back.'

'He died in my arms and I am going to kill Pontiff here right on the steps of his beloved courthouse and show this town that justice will be done, one way or another.'

She rammed the barrel of the pistol hard into Irish's back and pushed him forward toward the wide set of stairs to his right.

'Sue, that's *not* Pontiff,' said Skin.

They reached the outer edge of the ring of light cast by the group's lantern.

'Sue!' her father pushed forward toward her. 'I tell you, that is *not* Pontiff.'

She stood still, as if the announcement dazed her, and Irish spoke. 'It's true. I'm not even from this place.'

'It's that foreign fella. He's chubby, but he ain't no Pontiff.'

Despite his predicament, Irish squinted to see who had said that about him. He was hardly chubby. Babies are chubby. He was healthy, stout-hearted from all that walking in the wilderness.

'Who are you?' said Sue, in a low growl.

Before he answered, someone shouted, 'That's the one who shot Calvin.' There was a moment of suspended terror when everyone in the street paused and looked at everyone else. And Irish knew if he didn't act soon he would be killed. Whether he was mistaken for Pontiff or whether he was well and truly himself would not matter to this mob.

And then a little fat man emerged from the street's shadows, followed by Belle-Ruth. She held her pistol trained on the man's upper back, her right arm hanging limp at her side, the sleeve dark, her hand slick with her own dripped blood. The people in the street stared at the newcomers.

'Pontiff!' shouted Sue. She stepped out from behind Irish and raised the pistol. 'Whoever you are, get away from him. He's mine. I earned the right to kill him dead!'

'No. I aim to kill him. He killed my sister. He killed my Cheery.'

'He killed my Rip.'

'What?' said Pontiff. 'Rip? He's not — dead?'

Sue raised the pistol higher and said, 'If you don't move I'll shoot you, too, girl. Now get the hell away from Pontiff.' The words rushed from her like falling stones.

'No!' said Belle-Ruth, and moved forward. Irish spun his body toward Sue, his arm, heavy with the weight of momentum, swung upward, slashing at the pistol. The back of his hand connected with the cold steel, and he felt small bones snap. The gun went off and flew from the woman's hand, arcing up over their heads and landing in the dirt behind them. Irish ran for it. The woman growled and lunged at him, her teeth bared as if she might bite.

The group of men scattered. Irish grabbed the barrel of the pistol and dragged it through the gravel toward him. He backed away, to put distance between himself and the crowd.

'Stay back. I've no desire to shoot any of you, but so help me, harm a hair on that girl's head,' he jerked his head in Belle-Ruth's direction, 'and I'll let the first one of you have it.' He shook the pistol for emphasis, cradling his broken hand in his vest.

Irish saw the woman, Sue, clearly for the first time. She was a wild thing, like an escapee from the women's work-house in Tralina, up the west coast from his hometown in Ireland. Her hair flew about her face, her eyes lined red, her mouth still working in a sneer of anger, the teeth gritting and gnashing.

Belle-Ruth, careful to keep her captive between herself and the angry group, pushed Pontiff, who stumbled forward holding his arms in front of his chest as if he were clutching a bundle.

'Up the steps,' said Belle-Ruth.

'What are you going to do with me?'

'I'll do the talking,' she said, and jammed him hard in the back with the muzzle of the pistol.

They clunked and stumbled halfway up the steps. The worried noises of a nervous dog bubbled from Pontiff's throat. Belle-Ruth kept her body angled, the pistol poised to shoot Pontiff or at the crowd with equal ease.

Sue ran to her father. Irish wanted to tell her to stop but how could he? She was in need of solace. He didn't know any of these people but he knew they were her friends, and he knew they were all angry and hurt in one way or another. And so he let her retreat the few paces to the group.

Her sneer and angry gaze flashed to the two figures struggling up the stairs, then fixed on Irish. With no warning she lunged at her father's gun belt, whipped the pistol from its holster, and ran forward toward the stairs.

'No!' shouted Irish. The word echoed from other mouths on the street.

Three pistols flashed outside the courthouse. Through the drift of blue-gray smoke, Irish heard Sue shriek, saw her legs fold under her grimy dress, and she bent low to the ground, clutching her hands to her chest. Her father bent over her.

Pontiff was sprawled on the middle step, one knee under him, his mouth pulled tight and his hands clawed across the top of his head. Blood streamed between his fingers.

Belle-Ruth appeared to Irish to be much the same as she was before, pale and unsteady on her feet, and with one arm hanging limp and useless. Lord knew where her bullet went, thought Irish. For he knew his was the shot that had shattered Sue's brandished pistol.

He didn't think he'd hit her hand, but the impact and chunks of damaged wood and steel were enough to send a grown man to his knees. He'd hated to do it, but she left him no choice. She might have intended to shoot only Pontiff, but he couldn't take that risk, not with Belle-Ruth's life at stake.

Eyes were shifting to him, but he had to make sure Belle-Ruth got to the relative safety of the courthouse. It would at least buy them enough time to figure out what to do next.

'Belle, get in the courthouse!'

'I'm tryin', but he's fat and bleedin' and bawlin' like a new calf.'

Pontiff sobbed and tried to wedge the pudgy fingers of one hand between his neck and his tightening collar as Belle-Ruth pulled upward on his coat with all her effort. The pistol, in the same hand, wagged in his face. Irish thought that if Pontiff gained control of his senses he would snatch the gun from Belle's hand and that would be the end. Irish backed toward the alley while most eyes were on the two spectacles of Belle and Sue.

Belle managed to get Pontiff to his feet, despite the fat man's stuttering protestations. The crowd grew in size.

Irish guessed there were a half-dozen lanterns, and twice as many new faces, all confused, all looking in every direction, all at once. When Belle and Pontiff reached the courthouse door, Irish slipped back into the dark of the alley.

24

Mason leaned back against the door-frame, closed his eyes, and sighed. This was well and truly a mistake from the start. He never should have 'come out of retirement' as Rita called it. He had to admit to feeling his age more on this trip than on any other.

Since leaving life on the road behind and settling in with Rita at her way station a few hours' ride west of Kansas City, he was more satisfied than he'd been for years. It wasn't the little place she kept with its plain but familiar and even comfortable parts and pieces. Like the rawhide hinges on the winter privy door. They could afford steel pin hinges, but the others worked well enough. Or the grooves in the kitchen butcher block. Or that damned rooster, Pluck, who would not die. Like me, he thought, and smiled.

Maybe Rita's right. Maybe I already did what I can do and I should walk away from the past. Let it remain a dead thing. Maybe coming to Cayuse Falls was a mistake. He sighed and pushed away from the wall.

'Too late for that,' he said out loud and peeked around the door frame. No sense taking a bullet, and especially not for Pontiff. Not at this late date. He knew that he had too much to live for: the good woman who would, despite her threats to the contrary, still take him in when he returned from what she called his 'fool's errand.' The promises of things undone and those not yet tried were too great to ignore.

Mason's smile melted at the edges when he realized he had been with Rita longer than he had been with his Ruth. And he cursed the power of memory.

Shouts and three rapid shots whipped Mason from his reverie. He cursed himself for not paying attention to the task at hand. Just as well he was hanging up his trail gear — he'd never in all his time on the road allowed himself to lose track of his thoughts in a tense situation. He crouched low and peered around the door frame into the gloom of the still courtroom. The pleasant tang of fresh-planed pine filled his nose.

He sensed no one in the courtroom but himself and, sticking to the edges of the cavernous space, where the feeble shafts of moonlight hadn't yet worked their way in, he made his way to the front door. It was cracked; someone had either come in or out. Irregular lamp light and shouting voices sluiced through the parted doors. He didn't dare widen the gap, but he recognized Pontiff's voice, close by on the steps. He sounded like he was being gutted by Comancheros.

Mason had come a long way to make sure Pontiff got what he deserved and to sit inside like an old woman mending socks at the fire was too much to bear. He grunted and headed back the way he'd come. He'd slip outside and then see for himself what was left to do.

He turned to go and heard a woman's strained voice curse at someone outside the door. 'Get off your fat backside and get in there.' A high-pitched wailing responded. He heard a lilting voice, Irish, distant but unmistakable, say something about harming her head. He had to hand it to the little fella, he certainly knew how to rise to the occasion. Even if he bungled it most of the time.

Someone or something slammed against the door. The woman, he knew it was Belle-Ruth, was cursing more than ever. Had to be at Pontiff, he was the only one who could test a person's patience in such a way.

A shoulder, then a head and most of her torso appeared, widening the gap, and then Pontiff's head and collar, bloody hands squeezing his head. Belle-Ruth kept low and looked outside, afraid someone might pick her off. Mason reached down, grabbed a handful of collar, and dragged the little fat man straight into the courthouse foyer. Belle-Ruth stumbled backward and landed next to him at Mason's feet, who leaned over them and slammed the door shut.

'Hey! Oh, it's you,' said Belle-Ruth, backing away from Mason. 'He's mine,' she said. 'I owe Cheery. I want to make this bastard pay for what he done.'

'You're going to have to take a number, sister. This town is chock full of people who want to see this man dead.'

Pontiff whimpered and struggled to rise to his knees, his hands still clamped on his bleeding skull. Mason planted a boot on one of the chubby man's thighs and forced him back down to the floor. 'Keep still, Newie.'

Pontiff moaned.

'And shut your mouth,' said Mason.

Belle-Ruth stared at the big man like a cornered, starving dog.

'I'm not going to take your gun. I'm just making sure you stay alive.' He gestured at her shoulder. 'Irish said you were wounded. That arm looks bad. You should clean that up,' he said.

'I need advice, I'll ask for it.'

'If you live that long,' said Mason.

'What's that supposed to mean?'

'Means you're near to done in. The sooner we give these people what they want, the sooner you can get tended by a doctor.'

'Listen to him, Belle,' said a voice from the back of the room.

Mason's pistol found the exact spot the voice came from and the rapid clicks of the hammer cocking filled the cold, still air with finality.

Irish inhaled sharply, Belle stiffened, and even Pontiff stopped squirming long enough to look into the dark.

'Don't shoot, Mason. It's only me — Irish. Don't shoot.'

'Stop whining. You're as bad as Newie here.' Mason eased the hammer back down and holstered his pistol.

'Mind your own business, Irishman,' said Belle-Ruth, then her voice grew softer, 'I'll — ' She slumped against the wall, too weak to stand, her wounded arm cradled in her lap, her pistol gripped firmly in her other hand.

Irish rushed forward, bumping into benches and knocking down others. 'Belle,' he said, dropping to his knees in front of her. He tossed his pistol down, too close to Pontiff. And Mason moved too slow. Pontiff snatched up the pistol and grunted to his feet before Mason reached him.

'Newie,' said Mason. 'Do you even know how to use one of those things?'

'You shut up!' yelled the little bloody-headed man. 'I've had enough of you. Look at what you've done to me. To this town, all of the West, all afraid of the mighty Mason. All afraid you'll come after them. Well, I know the truth, Mason. I know all there is to know about you and you are a killer. A killer who must be put down.'

'And you think you're the man to do it?' Mason snorted in laughter.

'Shut up, Mason. I've had enough of your torment. I've paid whatever debt you think I owe. Long been paid. I've had enough and I'm going to end it all.'

Mason laughed again and in the back of the room, from the same corner from where Irish had emerged, a voice said, 'So you're Mason.'

Another joined in: 'And Pontiff knows him. I told you all.'

And from the front steps grew a loud clunking sound, and voices rose. Swinging lantern light shafted across the floor and someone kicked hard at the other closed door. At the same instant, the two men at the rear of the room advanced. Mason stepped backward, his hands hovering about his waist.

'That's far enough, Mason,' said one of the men. Mason stood still.

The front door crowded with a dozen people, and he heard more clumping up the steps behind them. A tall man with the rough, swing-armed look of a laborer stepped forward. The man looked around him, noted Irish and the still-unconscious Belle-Ruth, and said, 'Somebody want to tell us what's going on in our town? All we know is that everything was fine until you three strangers showed up.'

'That's right, Skin,' said Newie from his dark corner.

'Newie Pontiff! I should have known Sue's shot wouldn't kill you.' Skin Stropworth took a step toward Pontiff but Mason held out an arm and said, 'He's got a gun.'

'You're damned right I have,' said Pontiff, his voice quavering. 'No one comes closer. You hear?'

He angled around so that his back was to the vast empty room. Then he stepped to the left and groped the wall with a free hand. He swung a door open and slipped inside the stairwell to the clock tower.

It rose one flight and opened out onto the balcony before continuing on two more flights of winding stairs to the unfinished top, high above the peak. He stuck well to the shadows at the back of the space and was quiet, save for his labored breathing.

Mason walked up the aisle, slowly toward the bench at the head of the room. The territorial flag and the flag of the States hung side by side on poles on either side of the vast raised judicial bench.

'Hold it there, Mason,' said a man, followed by the snapping of a rifle levering.

Mason ignored the order and folded his arms across his chest. 'Well, Newland Pontiff. You've done pretty well for yourself here in Cayuse Falls.' He paused, but there was no sound save for the rasping breathing of the little man in the shallow balcony above them.

Mason turned from the bench and faced the room, his loud voice filling the quiet space. 'I guess you told these kind folks that when the time for statehood rolled around, why you'd make sure this town was well set up. All they had to do was be sure to build up a fine courthouse — this one'll do. Good, solid carpentering went into it. I dare say no small amount of money, too.' He looked at the people, all quiet, all willing to listen to what this man had to say, this famous killer of men and grim friend to the downtrodden.

'And then you found out about the railroad. Why, if ever there was an opportunity ready-made for a town — and for Newie Pontiff — it was that railroad deal. And the thing of it was, the railroad was practically begging him to be let right through your town. That is, if you all wanted it bad enough.'

Skin Stropworth said, 'How do you know all this, Mason? And why are you here?' He took a step forward, his big working-man's hands at his sides, gripping nothing but air, but wishing they were closing around someone's neck.

Mason held up a hand and said, 'I'm getting to that, pal. I'm here to tell you people that there isn't any railroad deal.'

The questioning voices and short, sharp shouts of anger forced Mason to hold his hands up. 'I know what Pontiff promised you. But he was lying. He's good at it. Been doing it for years. Hell, probably his whole life.'

'That's a lie!' shouted a ragged voice from the balcony.

'Oh, Newie, tell them the truth. For once, your honor. Honor — ha! Go ahead and tell them.'

'It's not true, I swear — '

The voices flooding the half-filled room rose to a shouting pitch.

'I knew it!' yelled a small, thin man in his shirtsleeves. 'You took us all for a ride!'

'Quiet! Quiet!' yelled Skin over and over until the room settled down. 'Before we go off half-cocked,' he turned to Mason. 'Why should we believe you, Mason? If that's who you are?'

'Well, now, I never said I was, and I never said I wasn't. And you can believe me,' he raised his voice and projected it toward the balcony. His voice became flat and hard. 'Because I was unfortunate enough, a long time ago, to be

Pontiff's business partner. And I trusted him. Like you did. And I've regretted it every day since then. And mister,' said Mason, looking at Skin, 'that's a pile of regret.'

'What'd he do to you?' said an old woman, pinching a shawl tight beneath her chin.

Mason drew in a deep breath. He nodded his head and looked around the room at all the expectant faces. 'A long time ago, when I was a young man, I was foolish enough to trust him. I'd come into some money from an uncle back East. It wasn't a fortune but it was enough for me and my wife, Ruth, and our baby girl. We bought our own little spread.' He smiled at the memory. 'A cuter place you'd never find.'

His smile faded and he said, 'Then Pontiff comes riding in one day, all fancied up, in a buggy and good-looking clothes. To make a long story short, one thing led to another and I found myself talked into signing over the rights to our place for a stake in a business venture. A certain thing, he told me. My wife, my Ruth, she warned me. But she knew my mind was made up and so, being the good woman she was, she didn't argue. I expect she thought I would have to learn this lesson, no matter how hard it turned out to be. And bless her, though she knew it she still stayed with me, right by my side.'

'Well, as you can imagine, we lost it all. And she never once told me she was right, never once reminded me of the terrible mistake I'd made in trusting him.' He swallowed, rasped a hand over his chin. The room was quiet, save for the shifting of feet, and the old woman blowing her nose softly.

'That wasn't enough for Pontiff. He thought I had more. Back in those days I used to call my daughter my little treasure. Hair as gold as her mother's and a heart of pure gold, too. Well, Pontiff thought I'd been talking of a real treasure all along, and he hired men to find it.' Mason's voice grew flat.

'Those men he hired left nothing to chance. No way anyone would ever connect them to the crime they committed.'

He pointed at the balcony and said, in a loud, solid voice, 'Those men killed my wife and daughter. With knives. And then they burned them in a house I no longer owned. All for a treasure that didn't exist.'

A full minute passed and the old woman said, in a low voice, 'How did you know it was Pontiff?'

A grim smile pulled at Mason's mouth and he said, 'I found those two men. And before they died they told me everything they knew. Every single thing. But Pontiff is nothing if not smart. He hid himself well. Moved from place to place. I was torn between paying my debts and finding him. I spent as much time as I dared tracking him down until I got the debt all paid off. And then I took to the road, tracking him full time.'

'Along the way I gained a reputation

as a man who helped people. Parts of that are fair, I guess. Hell, most of it was made up. I'm only a man, no more bloodthirsty than any other. By the time I caught up to him, he'd been sentenced to ten years in Exeter Prison for theft of jewelry, I think it was. Sound about right, Newie?'

There was no answer. Then they heard Pontiff say, 'You're telling lies. All lies!'

'Like hell I am,' said Mason. 'I decided to wait you out. But somehow you got released early. Some favor or other. Doesn't matter. You slipped through my fingers again, and then a few years later, I was talking with a friend of mine from the old days, Baxter Parker; we'd ridden together on and off. Now though, it might interest you to know, Newie, that he's with the Great Western and Overland Railroad.' He let the statement hang. 'That's right Newie. The very one you're so keen on for Cayuse Falls.'

A murmur rose in the room. 'I found

out that he was considering sending out scouts to a town near the Tilton Range. He said that an overbearing little man kept hounding him to visit his town, even though the place didn't sound all that promising. Man by the name of Newland Pontiff. You can imagine my surprise. The man I knew, the man who'd been directly responsible for the deaths of my family all those years before.'

Mason's voice was flat and hard. 'And in a show of typical arrogance, he was using the very name he had when I knew him. It was as if I was right back there at that smoldering ruin, pulling burnt timbers off the bodies of my family.'

★ ★ ★

For a handful of heartbeats no sound was heard, the last traces of Mason's speech diminished in the shadowed room. Then came soft, creaking sounds, like those of a rodent heard from another room. As they rose in volume, the gathered folks looked toward the balcony, toward the still-unseen Pontiff. It was his laughter that they heard, but a pinched, squeaking version of it, as though heard through a thin wall.

'You don't really expect the good citizens of Cayuse Falls to believe that paltry tale? You of all people? A known killer? An outlaw? Why, I'm surprised the people of my town haven't lynched you yet. They know when they're being hoodwinked, Mason. These people are much too smart to put up with any of your lies. They know the truth when they hear it, Mason!' His voice rose to a tremulous pitch.

Mason pictured the fat face, blood streaked from the parting his hair had received, staring out over them from the dark of the balcony.

'We know the truth when we hear it, Pontiff,' said Skin Stropworth. 'And it's something we ain't heard from you in a long, long time. Maybe never.' He jerked his chin at Scoot Flanders, who spun and headed for the balcony stairwell, but he stopped when Pontiff began shouting again.

'Mason! Mason, don't you leave me here! Don't you play me false, Mason! Wait, good people, you've only heard half the truth. Listen to me! Listen to my side of the story!' Again there was a pause. All eyes were on Mason. He looked up at Pontiff, then he shook his head and walked toward the front door.

★   ★   ★

Skin Stropworth led the charge toward the balcony stairs.

Pontiff shouted, 'No!'

They saw a dim outline of his shadowy bulk leaning over the rail. He fired two shots down into the dimly lit room, and a scream rose from the surging mob.

Pontiff stomped up the remaining two short flights of stairs to the top of the tower. There were no doors between him and the advancing crowd, but he did have the pistol with a few shots left. The mob had no head for such things.

Belle-Ruth leaned against Irish's shoulder and they followed Mason out the door. Even bent and huddling she was taller by a head than the little drummer. He supported her under her good elbow and with one arm about her waist. From behind them, terrible shouts rolled out the doors ahead of them, echoed above them, rained down at them.

There were but a handful of people still gathered in the street. Mostly couples and single folks, in a loose collective, some asking questions of the air, heads cocked and listening, some looking up at the jouncing lanterns and ascending figures in the skeletal, half-sheathed clock tower.

As Mason, Irish, and Belle-Ruth reached the bottom step, the few people left outside all looked up abruptly at the sound of shouting. Far above them the outline of Pontiff, skylined by the irregular lantern light of a pursuer from the stairs, slipped to his knees, struggled to his feet, only to lose his balance again as if he were being pulled. He barked and snarled, the garbled sounds of his curses reaching them far below.

He finally gained his feet and shouted down the ladder at the advancing citizens. His voice rang clear in the still, cloudless night, his squat body hunkered there, silhouetted in the moonlight. 'First one up outta that hole is going to see how mean ol' Newie can get.' He thrust the pistol at them as if he were pointing a finger in emphasis. 'I'm not fooling. You get back!' He thumbed the hammer.

'You know what's going to happen, don't you?' said Irish, close by Mason's shoulder, irritation in his voice. Yet they all looked up at the weird scene as if it were a play in a theatre on high. Mason didn't answer. Just watched.

'This is murder,' said Irish in almost a whisper, but he didn't look away. Belle stared skyward, the thought of a smile playing at the corners of her mouth.

'No! No!' Pontiff shouted, kicking at someone, something below him, one arm waving the pistol wildly. Then the glow of light appeared and there was a person up there with him. It was Skin Stropworth, holding a lantern. He moved toward Pontiff with an arm outstretched and yelled, 'Give me the gun, Judge.'

That last word had the power of a backhand to the fat man's face, and Pontiff flinched. He paused but a moment, then shook his head vigorously, waved the pistol at the man, and scrambled up onto the slight railing.

He shouted curses into the night, and grabbed blindly behind him for the corner post that supported the roof. He was perched, balancing on the top edge of the little railing, clutching the upright with one arm. He stretched to his full height then, and in the dim lantern light Mason swore he saw a smile on Newie Pontiff's face.

The little man faced the cold night air and spread his arms wide, his eyes closed and a smile on his face. Skin, standing behind him with the lantern held high, did not move forward. Pontiff dropped the pistol. It clunked against the railing, bounced once against the side of the building, then hit the ground.

'He's gonna jump!' shouted a boy no older than twelve, pointing toward the tower top, his other hand straining against his mother's tight grip.

'Oh, no, he ain't,' snapped Sue McCorkle as she shouldered her father's Winchester rifle. She squeezed off a shot so quickly no one on the ground knew quite what had happened. Less than a second later she levered another round, and sent it straight after the first — into the spasmed but still balanced body of Judge Newland Pontiff the Third.

One thin scream filled the night air from above. People twitched and gripped their loved ones tighter. And finally they stared at Sue, still holding aloft her father's smoking Winchester. They followed the barrel up to where it pointed, far above them.

The screams were from Pontiff, silhouetted against the moon-heavy sky, who had jerked fully upright, his arms flung wide, trying to hug the world. He remained there, impossibly still, for a few seconds, before falling forward as if he were a bat dropping for flight into the night. The long tails of his coat fluttered behind, then snagged on a jutting end of carpenters' bracing. His fat body followed its course, caught, and arced, slamming inward, head first. It hit the building, left something there against the fresh clapboards, and continued its long drop down. It landed before them with that air of finality they had grown to expect of Newland Pontiff's judicial decisions.

Far above them a handful of people, panting from their exertions, held tight to the corner posts and railings as they peered over the edge.

25

Mason turned and walked away from the crowd. Irish ran after him and grabbed the big man's sleeve, jerking him around. 'You knew this would happen! How could you let this happen?'

Mason, stone faced, looked down at the little man's bunched fist on his sleeve. He slowly lifted the hand away, then said, 'Everybody got what they wanted.' He turned and kept walking.

Irish stood still. 'But Pontiff is dead.'

Mason stopped and sighed, not turning back around. 'Like I said, everybody got what they wanted.' He took a step, then stopped. 'Take care, Irish. You're a good man.' Then he walked toward the livery.

'But — ' said Irish.

'Leave it be,' said Belle-Ruth, close beside him. And together they watched this man who was legend disappear into the chill night air.

THE END

We do hope that you have enjoyed reading this large print book.

Did you know that all of our titles are available for purchase?

We publish a wide range of high quality large print books including:
Romances, Mysteries, Classics
General Fiction
Non Fiction and Westerns

Special interest titles available in large print are:
The Little Oxford Dictionary
Music Book, Song Book
Hymn Book, Service Book

Also available from us courtesy of Oxford University Press:
Young Readers' Dictionary
(large print edition)
Young Readers' Thesaurus
(large print edition)

For further information or a free brochure, please contact us at:
Ulverscroft Large Print Books Ltd.,
The Green, Bradgate Road, Anstey,
Leicester, LE7 7FU, England.
Tel: (00 44) **0116 236 4325**
Fax: (00 44) **0116 234 0205**

Nogales was a hell town, in the heart of the desert. Its single claim to fame was its band of deadly guns-for-hire who lived there, especially Ryan Coder, whom some saw as the gun king. Yet Coder found his life on the line when he hired out to the king of Chad Valley and was pitted against Holly, the youngest and deadliest gunslinger of them all. Would Coder end up just another notch on Holly's gun?

THE DEVIL'S RIDER

Lance Howard

When vicious outlaw Jeremy Trask escapes the hangman's noose, he rides into Baton Ridge on a mission of revenge and bloodlust. It had been a year since he'd murdered manhunter Jim Darrow's brother in cold blood. Now, along with the sole survivor of the massacre, a young homeless widow named Spring Treller, Darrow vows to hunt down the outlaw — this time to finish him for good. But will he survive the deadly reception the outlaw has waiting?

SHOWDOWN AT PAINTED ROCK

Walt Masterson

When a wagon train is trapped by armed men in Painted Desert, mountain man Obadiah Peabody helps out. He believes they are all just another bunch of pilgrims aiming for California. But among the innocent travellers are the Driscoll brothers — the meanest bunch of owlhoots. Obadiah realises he's got a tiger by the tail when the brothers turn on their rescuer and kidnap his adopted granddaughter. Can Obadiah succeed against seemingly impossible odds? Can he even survive?

MISFIT LIL CLEANS UP

Chap O'Keefe

A senseless killing prevents scout and guide Jackson Farraday from investigating an odd situation in the Black Dog mining settlement. So he tricks Lilian Goodnight into spying at the High Meadows cattle ranch. Lil discovers range boss Liam O'Grady running a haywire outfit, crewed by deep-dyed misfits. She then finds she must rescue an ex-British army officer, Albert Fitzcuthbert, from renegade Indians. And Lil faces ever more problems that only her savvy, daring and guns can settle!